"Not every man you meet is a cheat and a liar."

"Not every man," Dinah agreed, "but a lot of them are. They use women for one reason or another and then chuck them away. Max was finished with me once I'd introduced him to everyone useful I knew." She looked at Quinn.

"And me?" he prompted.

"You know what you want!" It hurt to remember the real reason Quinn was interested in her. While his sensitive fingers had been caressing her, it had been easy to think that he wanted her for the oldest reason in the world.

"Yes, but do *you*?"

"You've made it blazingly obvious!"

"I thought so," Quinn agreed dryly. "But you showed no sign of getting my message."

"You want my program," she said, half wanting him to deny it.

Books by Charlotte Lamb

A VIOLATION

HARLEQUIN PRESENTS

412—MAN'S WORLD
417—STRANGER IN THE NIGHT
422—COMPULSION
428—SEDUCTION
435—ABDUCTION
442—RETRIBUTION
448—ILLUSION
451—CRESCENDO
460—HEARTBREAKER
466—DANGEROUS
472—DESIRE
478—THE GIRL FROM NOWHERE
528—MIDNIGHT LOVER
545—A WILD AFFAIR
585—BETRAYAL
635—THE SEX WAR
644—HAUNTED
658—A SECRET INTIMACY
668—DARKNESS OF THE HEART
700—INFATUATION
731—SCANDALOUS
747—A NAKED FLAME
762—FOR ADULTS ONLY
772—LOVE GAMES

HARLEQUIN ROMANCE

2083—FESTIVAL SUMMER
2103—FLORENTINE SPRING
2161—HAWK IN A BLUE SKY
2181—MASTER OF COMUS
2206—DESERT BARBARIAN

These books may be available at your local bookseller.

Don't miss any of our special offers. Write to us at the following address for information on our newest releases.

Harlequin Reader Service
P.O. Box 52040, Phoenix, AZ 85072-2040
Canadian address: P.O. Box 2800, Postal Station A,
5170 Yonge St., Willowdale, Ont. M2N 6J3

CHARLOTTE LAMB

love games

Harlequin Books

TORONTO • NEW YORK • LONDON
AMSTERDAM • PARIS • SYDNEY • HAMBURG
STOCKHOLM • ATHENS • TOKYO • MILAN

Harlequin Presents first edition March 1985
ISBN 0-373-10772-2

Original hardcover edition published in 1984
by Mills & Boon Limited

CHAPTER ONE

'YOU'RE jumpy today! Got a headache?' Angela asked as Dinah looked at the clock for the third time, her expression despairing. It had been one of those days when nothing seems to go right: the phone had never stopped ringing, people walked in and out of her office as though it was a short cut to Piccadilly Circus, and Angela had a cold which apparently made her deaf, since she kept asking Dinah to repeat what she had said clearly enough the first time.

'I haven't got time to dictate any more letters,' Dinah decided. 'Have you rung Adam Stuart's publicity people again?'

'Oh, sorry! I forgot,' Angela said and Dinah began to frown, until her secretary gabbled: 'I mean, yes, I did, but I forgot to tell you—he will do the programme.' She laughed as Dinah's face lit up.

'Oh, terrific! Off you go and get those letters typed, then. I'll be at the conference for the rest of the morning, remember.'

As the door closed behind Angela, Dinah took out a powder compact and looked at herself briefly, then ran a comb through her auburn hair, smoothed coral lip gloss on to her deceptively demure little pink bow of a mouth and lightly dusted her nose with powder. Her face was small, a clear calm oval which her vivid, fiercely alive green eyes contradicted; they dominated her features and were what people remembered about her.

She looked at the clock again and groaned, hurrying towards the door, only to trip over a metal wastepaper basket and lurch forward with a gasp of pain. The basket clattered across the room and Dinah swore. 'Damnation take the thing!'

Pulling up her straight, charcoal grey skirt she looked grimly at the ladder which had appeared in her tights. Wouldn't you know it? What else could go wrong today?

'I should have stayed in bed,' she thought aloud and somebody laughed. Dinah looked towards the door, startled. She should have guessed—who else would it be but Quinn Howard? He was studying her long legs with interest and Dinah crossly dropped her skirt and straightened, going pink.

'I heard what sounded like a fight so I came in to investigate,' he drawled.

'Sorry to disappoint you, Sherlock, I knocked over the wastepaper basket, that's all.' Dinah could still feel him staring at her and the deliberate nature of that assessment made her even more furious, partly because she knew he was aware of her irritation and amused by it. Quinn Howard was a supremely self-aware man with a cool, controlled mind, and what Dinah regarded as a perverted sense of humour. He seemed to enjoy teasing her and her efforts at keeping her temper simply added to his fun.

Quinn was one of the male lobby in the

company who wanted her out of her job. He might be eyeing her figure now, but it was her programme Quinn Howard was really after, and Dinah bristled as she stared back at him.

'Got your proposals ready?' he asked, looking at her empty hands as she moved towards him and Dinah stopped in her tracks.

'Yes, of course,' she said, turning back to snatch up the folder from her desk. She had spent the past week painstakingly preparing the detailed proposals for the autumn schedule. How on earth had she come to forget them? It was Quinn Howard's fault, of course. The man was a jinx; whenever he was around he made her jittery. She felt him watching her now with that cool, ironic smile, as if everything about her made him laugh, and the only way she could cope with his air of private amusement was to pretend she didn't notice it. The trouble was that she spent so much energy in appearing to be unaware of him that it made her inwardly on edge in his company.

'What exciting plans do you have for the autumn?' he asked as they headed for the lift.

'You'll find out soon enough.' Dinah meant to hold her fire until the last moment. It didn't make her any better tempered when she saw her secretary smile dreamily at him, as they passed her in the corridor. It didn't surprise Dinah, either, of course—Angela was a romantic, susceptible girl who was blind to everything but Quinn Howard's good looks.

A loose-limbed, elegant man he moved with a boneless grace which was both lazily casual and close to being hypnotic, judging by the reaction he got from Angela every time she set eyes on him. Dinah had soon realised that her secretary thought he was the best thing since sliced bread, but if Quinn Howard had charm it left Dinah cold, she was far too conscious of the ambitious mind behind his blue eyes. It maddened her that he lost no chance to remind her that she was a woman. Some women might have been flattered by his attention; ever since he joined the company he had been watching her and Dinah had been averting her eyes from him, prickling with antagonism, because that permanent sexual appraisal went hand in hand with an unhidden determination to get her job.

Quinn pressed the lift call button and leaned against the wall, surveying her thoughtfully.

'You look like someone getting ready for a war.'

'Are you surprised? You and your friends fight me over everything I suggest,' Dinah said, her chin lifted belligerently.

'You take it all too seriously. The idea of the conference is to give everyone a chance to discuss what everybody else is doing, it helps to iron out problems if ideas are kicked around by the whole team.'

Dinah smiled angrily. 'Oh, that's the theory— but the practice is something else again. What actually happens is that the men gang up to nod their own proposals through and then get down to the fun of tearing my ideas to shreds.'

Quinn's mouth twisted. 'Did anyone ever tell you that you had eyes like a cat?' He stared down into them, a good head taller than her and leaning far closer than she liked, his face only inches away. Her green eyes grew hectic with resentment. They *were* catlike, she admitted, but did not like the admission; they slanted, as bright as green glass, crowded with private thoughts which she hid by dropping her lashes.

'That's right, change the subject—but I notice you didn't try to deny what I'd said!'

'You need a holiday,' was all he answered. She knew the comment didn't indicate concern for her; only yet another way of getting at her, suggesting that she wasn't up to doing her job. 'You're overworked,' Quinn added. 'If you're not careful you'll burn out and then. . . .'

'Then you'll get my job?' she interrupted fiercely. 'Don't be too hopeful—I've no intention of cracking under the strain.'

The lift doors opened and a secretary emerged, getting out of Dinah's way with an inaudible apology as she saw the expression on Dinah's face.

I will *not* lose my temper, Dinah thought, marching into the lift. I *will* keep calm. Whenever Quinn Howard was around she found herself behaving aggressively, he put her back up with every other word and as for that smile of his . . . Dinah couldn't stand the sight of it. Nobody likes being laughed at and she knew that there was laughter in those blue eyes when they stared at her.

'Don't lose your temper so early in the game or we'll really have fireworks later,' Quinn advised softly as the lift doors closed on them.

Dinah jabbed the sixth floor button and the lift

began to rise. She stared at the steel wall, her face rigid.

'Going to Mark's party tonight?' Quinn enquired, apparently oblivious of the fact that she was ignoring him.

'I suppose so,' she reluctantly muttered. Mark's parties were royal command performances. Everyone was expected to show up if they got an invitation and it was recognised that being on the invitation list was a sure sign of rising status in the company. An invitation was a coveted status symbol; people hoped eagerly to get one and a failure to do so was an indication either that you were not one of the inner circle or that, if you had been, you had offended Mark in some way and might as well resign before he found an excuse to sack you.

'You've known him for years, haven't you?' Quinn asked and she looked round at him, frowning.

'Is that a hint that I got my job through influence?'

'It was a simple question, nothing else. Why are you so touchy? You have more prickles than a hedgehog.'

The lift stopped and they left it to walk down to the conference room. Dinah sat down at the long, polished table and Quinn took the seat opposite her, watching as she glanced through her thick folder of notes. She did not look up although she was aware of him. His face was often contradictory; one minute alive with restless, dynamic energy and the next calmly in repose and attentive to whatever was happening around him. Dinah found him far too disturbing as an opponent. He made her feel that she needed all her own wits and energy to match him. She could cope with all the other men, but Quinn worried and tired her. She had known on sight that he was going to be a threat to her.

'So how long have you known Mark?' he pressed.

Looking up, she said flatly: 'Since I was at school. He came to give us a talk on television when I was in the sixth form and I sat next to him afterwards at the special tea the school laid on for him. He offered me a job as a secretary and I jumped at it.'

'You've come a long way since then, haven't you? How long ago was that?'

'Seven years. He made me a research assistant when I was twenty.'

Quinn pursed his lips in a whistle, staring.

'Then I did a variety of jobs on the studio floor for a couple of years and ended up as an assistant producer when I was twenty-three.'

'A fast-moving career,' Quinn observed drily, just as the door opened and Mark walked in followed by a troop of other men who took their seats around the long table as soon as Mark had sat down.

There was a distinctly mischievous streak in Mark Woodstock's nature; he enjoyed stirring up trouble on occasions like these and then sitting back to watch the fun. As he met Dinah's eyes now he grinned and winked. She might not be looking forward to the next hour or two, but Mark clearly was.

Metro was a small commercial television station based in London, with an audience viewing figure ranging upward to several million at peak time for certain programmes, and Mark had built it up almost single-handed, being both managing director and one of the larger shareholders in the company. His word was law; he had the board in the hollow of his hand and always got his own way. He took risks when he felt it would pay off, and his programme planning had both originality and flair because he picked people who had both qualities. It was because Mark was a gambler with a daring nature that he took risks with people, as he had with Dinah; surrounding himself with young, ambitious and often daringly inventive producers whose lack of experience would have told against them with any other company. Mark worked them hard, for long hours, it was exhausting but it gave them a rapid education in programme making at all levels, which in turn made them professional and enthusiastic about their work.

A very thin, nervously alive man with bright dark eyes and a bushy head of dark brown hair springing with leonine vitality from his high forehead, Mark was barely forty himself, and as obsessed with television as he expected his employees to be, which made him a formidable boss. He had forgotten more about television than most of them had learnt and they were all aware of it. He was feared and respected and regarded warily. None of them ever had the chance to feel safe, to get staid and self-satisfied. Dinah knew that if Mark decided she had lost her touch he would drop her without a second thought.

The offices stood on the north bank of the river Thames, within a stone's throw of London Bridge, with a view of the crowded city skyscape from the conference room window on one side, and on the other a vista of the gunmetal grey river winding far below, with white modern buildings and dark wharfs lining the far bank. Dinah did not have to look to see, she knew the view by heart, just as she was familiar with the conference room with its long mahogany table and portrait of the Queen on one wall, and the pale beige carpet, which you could see everywhere in the building, since all the offices were decorated in a uniform style, except where a few more human touches had begun to appear as secretaries imported plants in pots and colourful posters to pin on their office walls.

'How's our golden girl today?' Mark asked her, smiling wickedly, and Dinah smiled back without answering, knowing that Mark was deliberately setting out to annoy everyone else in the room by making much of her.

'I hope we're going to win another Star Award this year,' Mark said, looking at the wall behind Dinah. Along the wall hung plaques and glittering golden stars in a neat row, awards won by the station during the previous years. Dinah had won two of them for her programme, which had been innovative and challenging from the very beginning.

'We'll try,' Dinah said, her hands on the folder in front of her, and all the men looked down at the folder, as if trying to guess its contents. Dinah had kept her plans a closely guarded secret, she didn't want to give any of her rivals a chance to steal her thunder or work out ways of attacking her ideas.

'One Nation' had been a phrase which stuck in her mind as she travelled around London during her early years at the station, seeing the violent contrasts in the city between rich and poor, young and old, black and white, and when Mark asked her one day what sort of programme she would make if she had a free hand she had put up the idea of a series based on the divisions in the way society worked, each programme contrasting two particular sections of society. Mark had listened attentively then told her he would let her make a pilot programme; a one-off half-hour programme which must be tightly costed and kept to the lowest possible budget.

'Are you serious?' she had asked, hardly believing it, and he had laughed at her wide-eyed excitement, pleased by it. Mark liked enthusiasm and commitment among his staff. That first programme had been made on a shoestring budget, with a very small camera crew and herself writing and producing it although one of the staff interviewers had been brought in to do the actual interviews with the public. In a real sense it had been Dinah's view of Britain; passionate, personal and, she now realised, rather young and naive, but whatever the faults and flaws in the programme it had caught the public attention and letters had poured in from all over London. Mark had repeated the programme a few weeks later and had told Dinah to go ahead and make another six.

'Six?' the other producers had echoed when they heard about it. 'You'll never get six programmes out of it; you've used up the material now.'

Dinah had smiled sweetly. 'We'll see,' was all she had said and gone on to make the proposed series as successfully as she had made the pilot programme. That autumn she won her first Gold Star Award. Mark had been delighted; the other producers had been politely reticent. Smiling tightly they had congratulated her and then spent the next few months trying to edge her programme out of peak time and preferably out of the schedules altogether.

The following year she won a second Gold Star Award for a programme about old people and teenagers. A few weeks later Quinn Howard had joined the company to make a monthly arts magazine programme and a few programmes on current affairs, and since his arrival all Dinah's opposition had been centred around him. Quinn had a tongue like a scorpion when he chose; could sting viciously and smile blandly all at the same time and once the others realised that he somehow got under Dinah's skin they sat back to enjoy the battle of wits into which every conference now developed.

A willowy young secretary had arrived with Mark's jug of water and a glass. Mark sipped, smiled benevolently and said: 'Shall we start, then? Eric, what are your plans?'

Eric was a short, stout man in his late fifties

whose programme never varied; he did a gardening programme which had an enormous adult audience and while he droned on most people drew doodles on blotting paper or stared out of the window, waiting for the real fun to begin.

Mark deliberately left Dinah's proposals to the last and when she opened her folder everyone sat up, wide awake and alert. She sold her ideas with her usual passionate conviction but she knew they were all merely waiting for her to stop talking so that they could get out their knives.

'Thank you, Dinah,' Mark said when she looked up defiantly in the silence that fell as she stopped reading. 'Comments, anyone?' And then before they could all yell at the same time, 'Quinn?'

Quinn was rolling a pencil between finger and thumb, his expression thoughtful. 'I seem to remember that you did a programme on immigrant populations as one of your first six programmes?'

'Yes, I did but I want to go into it more deeply this time, I. . . .'

'It's a mistake to cover the same ground twice,' Quinn said and the other men made noises of agreement, nodding. 'And the programme on retirement comes close to being a re-run of the programme contrasting the attitudes of young and old, I'd guess—if you're following the established programme theme—then you must be contrasting retirement with something but you made no mention of that aspect.'

'Tired ideas,' someone muttered.

'You don't want to get stale,' Quinn said. 'You've a brilliant reputation as an originator and if you're not careful to move on into new fields you're in danger of becoming an institution churning out the same ideas over and over again.'

'Quinn's right.'

'Absolutely.'

'Couldn't agree more, what I've been saying for months.'

'Here, here.'

Dinah ignored the voices coming from all sides of her, she concentrated on Quinn's cool, watchful face, her colour high and her green eyes flashing with temper.

'I think at least four of my proposals are completely new and challenging.' She outlined them again briefly, stressing the fact that the station had never covered those particular subjects.

'Too controversial,' someone said, and Eric woke up with a snort and nodded, looking dazedly amiable. The man beside him had just dug him in the ribs to indicate that his agreement was needed.

Dinah deliberately looked at him. 'What do you think, Eric?'

He rolled his eyes around nervously. 'Er ... too controversial,' he repeated, 'Offend the public.'

'What will?' Dinah challenged.

He looked at Quinn like a drowning man clutching at a very substantial straw. It was obvious to them all that Eric had no idea what they had all been talking about; he spent a lot of his time in the open air and offices made him sleepy.

'You need to do something new,' Quinn said, changing the subject. 'It's time you moved on, Dinah. Two years ago you were doing exciting, novel stuff but now you're scraping the barrel for ideas. The series should be terminated; it has done its job, and a remarkable job too, nobody wants to knock you or your programme but two years is a good run. You need a change; you're tired, your programme is tired.'

Another man leant forward, his sharp face caught in the morning sunlight from the high windows. 'You need a long holiday, Dinah,' he said soothingly. 'I think you look exhausted.'

She smiled icily. 'You can't have it both ways—if one of my proposals is controversial I can't be offering stale ideas. You'd better make up your minds.'

'One swallow doesn't make a summer,' murmured John Mower, the head of the news department. He and Dinah often clashed because John felt she was taking ideas his department could use, hunting over his territory. 'One good idea doesn't warrant an eight-programme series.'

The head of current affairs nodded, his head propped on his two hands and his elbows on the table. 'Personally I'm bored with the series, I don't know about the public but I wouldn't mind betting that they are too.'

Mark flipped open his folder and read out the programme's audience figures. Dinah coolly watched the men's faces; nobody said anything for a minute, looking sulky, then Quinn drawled:

'However good her viewing figures, Dinah has done the programme single-handed for two years, putting out how many programmes? Twelve? Sixteen? The original idea was good but she can't go on forever harping on one theme without burning out.'

'Do you feel tired?' Mark asked Dinah in a concerned tone, his eyes laughing.

'No,' she said through her teeth.

'Burnt out?' he enquired.

'Not in the least!' she snapped. 'And I'm still waiting to discuss my actual proposals in detail—instead of sitting here listening to all this nonsense about the programme being stale. How many programmes has Eric done? Why hasn't anyone suggested that he's exhausted and on the verge of burning out?'

Eric woke up, face startled. 'What? What's that?'

Dinah threw a hand towards him, smouldering with fury. 'I rest my case,' she said as Eric blinked at them all, totally at sea, and visibly worried by what he wasn't sure he had really heard. Eric's programme followed a well-worn track with a content that rarely varied, but his audience was quite happy with that and nobody had ever hinted to Eric that he might try a new approach.

'Now what about this Adam Stuart pro-gramme?' Mark asked in an amused voice and the conference got down to discussing Dinah's proposals in more detail.

They broke for lunch at half-past one, by which time everyone was in a bad mood, including Eric who was on edge with impatience to get to the pub before it shut. Mark watched Dinah gathering up her papers as the others rushed out of the room.

'You should be flattered, you know—if you weren't so good at your job they wouldn't bother with you. Take it as the compliment it is; don't let them get to you.'

Dinah looked up, very flushed, and caught a glimpse of Quinn Howard in the doorway, looking back at them with narrowed, watchful eyes. 'It's not because I'm good at my job,' she said, her voice projected towards him and quivering with anger. 'It's because I'm a woman! I'm the token woman on your team, aren't I, Mark? If you had more women producers they wouldn't pick on me all the time. You have women floor managers and research assistants but I'm the only producer and don't tell me that's pure coincidence.'

Quinn walked out as Mark frowned. 'You can't seriously suspect me of prejudice against women producers? I picked you, didn't I? I want to have the best people I can get, I don't care what sex they are but this is a small station and by sheer coincidence so far the right person for a particular job has always been a man.'

Dinah walked slowly towards the door and he followed her. Over her shoulder Dinah muttered: 'Some would say that that is stretching coincidence too far!'

Mark said impatiently: 'I don't know why you're getting so uptight. So they gave you a rough ride! I like a lively conference—it shows they're all awake and interested.' He paused, laughing. 'Except Eric and even he showed some signs of life once or twice. Very naughty of you to tease him, though; poor Eric hasn't much of a sense of humour.'

'None of them have,' snapped Dinah, and paused at the lifts, pressing the button.

Mark gave her a downward, impatient stare, propping himself up against the wall with one hand. 'You seem to have mislaid your sense of humour, too.'

'I get a little tired of being a shooting gallery with everyone aiming at me,' she said. 'I have to work twice as hard as the rest of them because I'm well aware that the minute I slip, even a fraction, the whole pack of them will go for me.'

'Maybe Quinn is right, maybe you're under too much pressure,' he said, staring at her with a concerned frown. The lift arrived and Dinah walked into it. Mark stood in the corridor, his hands thrust into his pockets, watching her, his thin body briefly at rest. 'Coming to my party tonight?' he asked in a voice which expected an affirmative answer, and Dinah drily gave him what he expected, her mouth wry.

'Of course.'

'That's what you need, I think—a little fun. You work too hard, it's getting to you.' A wicked spark lit in his often mournful dark eyes. 'Women aren't used to executive pressures, that's the trouble—they can't take it like the men.'

He was deliberately baiting her, and Dinah refused to rise to it this time. She gave him a sarcastic smile, pressed the second floor button and said: 'See you,' as the lift doors began to close. She caught the disappointment in his expression as he vanished from sight; Mark loved a good fight, he had a teasing combatative nature.

Dinah often suspected that his private life was rather lonely these days. He had been married for twelve years when his wife died unexpectedly on an operating table during minor surgery. It should have been perfectly straightforward but for some inexplicable reason her heart had failed and she never regained consciousness. The shock had aged Mark overnight. Dinah vividly remembered the long months during which he had been a grim, unsmiling figure who rarely spoke. She had been an assistant producer and had seen him around frequently; often he didn't seem to remember who she was and walked past without so much as a glance. He had slowly climbed out of that slough of depression; it was almost four years since his wife's death, but he hadn't shown signs of interest in anyone else. He had a son who was thirteen and away at boarding school most of the year, and a housekeeper who came for a few hours every weekday to keep the house in good order. Mark's life seemed to revolve around his work.

When she got back to her office Dinah locked away her detailed programme proposals in the steel filing cabinets along the wall behind her desk. She meant to rush down to snatch a quick lunch in a restaurant opposite the Metro building. She was about to leave when she heard Angela giggling in the tiny office next door, and then Quinn's voice followed by more giggling from her secretary.

Dinah pulled open the door and they both looked round at her, startled. Angela switched off her smile and started typing hurriedly. Quinn slid off her desk, on which he had been perched, bending over Angela as he talked, and sauntered towards Dinah, who eyed her secretary sharply.

'I hope those letters are going to be ready by five-thirty.'

'Oh, yes,' Angela said a little breathlessly, her buttercup blonde curls faintly dishevelled as though she—or someone else—had just run their fingers through them.

Dinah walked back into her own office and Quinn followed, closing the door behind him. The rattle of Angela's typewriter diminished in volume but did not halt.

'Don't distract my secretary from her work, she has enough trouble concentrating without you around,' Dinah said tartly and Quinn looked amused.

'Distracting? Is that what I am? How flattering.'

'It wasn't meant to be,' Dinah said, not liking the look in his mocking blue eyes.

'I distract you, do I?' Sunlight gleamed on his thick, dark hair as he moved his head to look down at her, suddenly far too close. Dinah stared at his straight, classical nose which gave his features a touch of arrogance and in profile made his face as striking as a face on a coin. Her own small, tiptilted nose annoyed her, she couldn't help admiring Quinn's classic features and that annoyed her, too. She didn't want to admire anything about him; he was her rival, a dangerous opponent, and she couldn't afford to have any weak spots where he was concerned.

'Don't bother trying to flirt with me,' she said, lifting her chin in her characteristic gesture of defiance. 'Angela may fall for your line but it leaves me cold.'

'Everything leaves you cold, you little icicle,' Quinn said, his mouth twisting in mockery, and her colour heightened.

She turned her back on him deliberately. 'Pull it out for me, would you? I can't reach.'

'What are you talking about now?' he asked, baffled.

'The knife you planted in my back during the conference,' she said, swinging round again to meet his eyes, her own bright angry green.

His brows met, and his mocking mouth tightened. 'Dinah, you're becoming paranoid. Every whisper of criticism is treated like black treachery, you see enemies behind every bush and you've lost all sense of humour and proportion. You're overworked, can't you see that? For the past two years you've been straining every nerve to keep up the high standard you set yourself with that first programme and you've done it brilliantly, nobody wants to take that away from you. Mark thinks the sun shines out of you, the board adores you, your career is one big success story, but you're living on your nerves and you can't keep it up much longer. Sooner or later, you're going to crack. Why not admit you're human and take a month off; get right away from Metro, relax, lie in the sun and vegetate for a few weeks, forget about your programme and the station and whether your ratings are staying high, forget everything and just enjoy living for a while?'

'Oh, you'd love that,' she said tersely. 'And while I was away, who would be making my first programme? It goes into production in three weeks and I still have all the groundwork to do on it, who would cope with it while I was away if not you? Don't try to kid me, Quinn. I know what you're after.'

He considered her with unmistakable irony. No doubt he had persuaded himself that he had cloaked that ambition of his with charm, he wouldn't believe that she could see right through him.

'You know what I'm after, do you?' he asked, his mouth amused.

'You may think you're very clever, but you aren't kidding me!' Dinah threw back at him, her eyes icy. 'I know why you're always trying to undermine me.'

'I doubt that. You're too myopic—you aren't seeing anything very clearly at the moment, that's your whole problem.'

'I see you—as clear as crystal! I've met your type before, I'm immunised, you'll never pull the wool over my eyes!'

'Have you now?' he said in an altered tone, his eyes suddenly bright and watchful. 'When was that? And what did he do to you?'

Dinah was taken aback by the question, and the perception which had prompted it, her eyes flickering away as she tried to think of an evasive answer. How on earth had he caught on to that?

She had spoken without thinking, never suppos-
ing that she might betray anything, but she
should have remembered that Quinn Howard was
a damned sight too astute to be taken lightly.

'That's right,' she said sharply. 'Try to make it
personal, whatever the subject it has to centre
around sex, doesn't it? We wouldn't want to give
women the idea that they might actually be able
to think as well as any man, would we?' She
turned away before he could answer that and
walked to the door. 'You may not have anything
better to do than stand around here making light
conversation, but I'm busy,' she said as she went
out, letting the door slam behind her. If Quinn
followed, he moved too slowly. Dinah ran down
the stairs instead of waiting for the lift and made
her way out of the building across the road to the
small restaurant just in time to have lunch before
they stopped serving it.

The restaurant was almost empty; she found a
table in a corner and looked gloomily at the menu
while the waitress hovered next to her, chewing
gum and reeling off a list of items which were no
longer available. Dinah sighed and eventually
ordered a cheese salad but when it came it was
limp and tired, the cheese a mere scattering of
grated Cheddar with the texture of granite chips.
Dinah's appetite was almost nil by then; she ate
some of the lettuce and tomato and a roll,
pushing the plate away.

Quinn Howard had reminded her of the man
she most wanted to forget; she hadn't allowed
herself to think of Max for two years, merely
remembering him made her feel humiliated and

depressed. At the back of her mind, somewhere, she had always linked the two of them although she hadn't consciously been aware of it. Quinn didn't resemble Max physically, what they had in common was less tangible, those cool, ambitious minds disguised by charm and good looks.

Dinah had been three years younger—and far more impressionable—when she met Max. She had had an occasional boyfriend but her sophistication and sexual experience had been very limited, she hadn't seen past Max's smile and smooth expertise with women. She had been too busy falling violently in love to realise that Max's interest in her was not basically romantic; he wanted to get into television not into her bed, although he was prepared to use her bed as a halfway house. Max had been an actor, an unsuccessful one, glad to get jobs doing modelling or demonstrating new gadgets in department stores. He had wanted to get into television commercials, that was where he could earn big money, he felt, and meeting Dinah at a party and discovering that she worked at Metro he had pursued her eagerly.

It had been a clever campaign. Looking back, she saw that now, but at the time it had fooled her completely. Max had sent her red roses and taken her breath away, he had taken her out to dinner and walked home with her afterwards, holding hands while he told her he loved her and they paused to watch the yellow lamplight glinting on the dark water of the river. He had looked down into her dreamy eyes and said things that made her shiver with delight but even his passion had been faked although she hadn't realised it. He didn't rush anything; it was weeks before he got around to dropping gentle hints. Dinah had even thought that it was her own idea to introduce him to people at Metro. She had been so happy to show him off to her friends; she was too crazy about him to suspect his intentions, it had seemed natural to take him to parties, drop his name to people.

Her obsession with him had made her neglect her own career for a while, Mark had made some tart comments and warned her to put more energy into her job and less into her private life. She had tentatively mentioned it to Max, expecting him to protest but he had been surprisingly acquiescent; at the time she had admired him for telling her she ought to see less of him for a while, her work was as important as his own, she mustn't risk it by burning the candle at both ends.

Dinah saw less of him over the next month and began to worry; she rang him and he made excuses, he was very busy, he was just going out of town, he had a touch of flu. Each time the reason was different and each time she accepted it, but with increasing uncertainty and a sense of hurt pride. She knew he was working regularly on television commercials, gossip like that soon got around, but it was a stark shock to hear at last that he was having an open affair with a well-known television actress. It was even more of a shock to realise that everyone had known about it for some weeks and hadn't mentioned it to her because they were sorry for her.

Nobody told her the truth; she had picked it up in brief fragments from snatches of talk she overheard, an occasional newspaper story when Max got a small part in the TV star's new series. Max himself had vanished from her life, her friends discreetly avoided mentioning him, Dinah pretended she had forgotten his existence. She could not have borne to talk about him, it wounded her pride to know that she had been used with such ruthless opportunism, she preferred to pretend that they had parted by mutual agreement. She tried not to think about him; her humiliated realisation of her own folly and his phoney lovemaking made it too painful. Once the original ache had stopped hurting she had been able to see Max for what he was, a man on the make and using her emotions to trick her into helping him become successful. He had been part of her education; her anger with herself had been channelled into her own career. Looking back she could see that her drive and fire when she was making her very first award-winning programme could all be traced back to the anger she had felt over Max; in that sense, perhaps he had been as useful to her as she had undoubtedly been to him, but Dinah felt no gratitude for that.

Max had taught her to take a microscope to the motives of any man who came near her and she wasn't going to let another man make a fool of her, certainly not someone like Quinn Howard.

CHAPTER TWO

DINAH left the office early that evening in order to go back to her London flat and change before going on to Mark's party. Angela caught her just as she was about to leave and announced anxiously: 'I couldn't get a camera team for the weekend when Adam Stuart is in England—shall I try one of the freelance agencies?'

Dinah paused, frowning. 'What a nuisance! That will put the cost up and the budget for that programme is tight enough already.' She considered for a second, her green eyes rueful, then shrugged. 'Oh, go ahead! I must have Stuart, he's a big enough fish to warrant the cost. He rarely visits England and hates being interviewed, it will be a scoop and I'm sure I can sell the extra cost to Mark.'

Angela dithered, her blonde hair clinging to her flushed forehead. High summer had arrived unexpectedly during the afternoon, London was sweltering in heat and everyone was complaining.

'Would you rather wait until you can talk to Mark?' Her hesitant tone suggested that Mark might be angry when he heard that they were having to get a freelance camera team instead of using one of their own. No doubt she was right, Mark would hit the roof, but Dinah bristled at being warned so openly by her secretary. She had already recognised the risk and discounted it;

Mark's first reaction would soon calm down to a resigned acceptance of the position, he knew how reluctant their cameramen were to work at weekends.

'I'll deal with Mark,' Dinah said sharply. 'You get on to the agencies now. Try Patrick first; his work is always good, even if he is expensive.'

'Okay,' Angela agreed in a voice which said: well, it's your funeral, and Dinah walked past her out of the office, smouldering. Angela was a good secretary and Dinah liked her, but Angela's only real ambition was to get married, she had no serious interest in her work. She refused to make it the centre of her existence, which you had to do at Metro if you wanted to get promotion. There was a well-trodden path from secretary to research assistant and upward. Dinah had taken that way herself, she put all her energies into her work and could not understand Angela's apathy. It irritated her that Angela always shot off dead on five-thirty and was never available for overtime at weekends or for any special project out of office hours. Half the time Angela didn't remember details in the forward planning of the programmes, she wasn't excited by what she was doing or what was going on around her, she merely went through the motions, did what she was told to do and no more.

Her secretary's attitude made life difficult for Dinah at times, she couldn't trust Angela to do anything on her own initiative, Dinah had to keep a permanent eye on her, and from time to time she considered asking for a new secretary. She did not do so because she liked Angela, in spite of her indifference to her job; she knew she might get someone far worse whom she liked less. Sooner or later Angela would no doubt be getting married to one of the men she seemed to keep on a string, which would take the decision out of Dinah's hands.

Dinah caught a bus to her flat and had to stand all the way because at five o'clock the rush hour was in full flood, people crammed into buses and underground trains like sardines, sweating in the heat, bad-tempered and tired, carrying their jackets over their arms because the sudden heat wave had caught them unawares.

Dinah was hungry, the smell of celery in the bag of a woman standing next to her made her nostrils quiver and her stomach heave. She had barely touched that salad, she would have to grab a quick meal before she went on to Mark's party. He would have a few plates of delicacies scattered around but they wouldn't be very filling. She was regretting having worn her charcoal grey skirt, the waistband was a tight hand around her flesh and her silk blouse was sticking to her back in this heat. She would be glad to get out of her clothes and take a cool shower.

She expected to find her flat empty but when she put her key in the door she heard Beth humming in the kitchen. Walking into the room Dinah grinned at her enquiringly. 'Skipped your tutorial?' Beth was in her second year at London University, studying Modern Languages; at this time of day each Friday she should be having her tutorial, a weekly treat to which she looked forward with all the enthusiasm of a martyr going to meet the lions.

'The curse finally fell on him,' Beth said cheerfully, scooping baked beans on to two thick slices of buttered toast, a calorie laden feast at which Dinah gazed with ravenous envy. She hadn't eaten butter for months, it put pounds on her hips, but Beth ate what she liked and didn't gain an ounce, it simply wasn't fair. 'He picked up a tummy bug in Italy and is staying in bed for the next week. I won't be seeing him next week, either. Now I know there's a God.'

Dinah looked around the cluttered kitchen. 'Did you make all this mess cooking beans on toast?'

Her sister shrugged casually, tossing back hair the colour of melting marmalade, a streaky mixture of blonde and red. Sitting down at the tiny kitchen table she began to eat, talking with her mouth full in the way their mother had insisted they never should 'I'll clear it up.'

When Beth won a scholarship to the college which was only a bus ride from Dinah's flat it had been inevitable that she should move in with Dinah since their parents lived in Essex, too far out to make a daily train journey practicable. Dinah's flat was small, the sisters had to share a bedroom, Beth never had any money and was addicted to studying with loud pop music playing, but they had worked out a scheme for living gradually. Dinah bought Beth a pair of earphones so that she could listen to her music without Dinah having to do so too, Beth had her own cupboard for food so that she could cook her own meals unless Dinah offered to share whatever she was cooking, Beth paid a tiny amount towards the rent and was supposed to tidy up after she had entertained or been cooking. Dinah had drawn up these rules after one week of having her sister in the flat; Beth must organise herself or get murdered, she told her firmly. After years of living alone Dinah had found a constant presence in her home distinctly irritating.

Beth was untidy, noisy, given to sudden glooms of depression or euphoric outbursts of excited emotion. She left her books, clothes, records scattered all over the flat. Half the time it was Dinah who picked them up, exhausted by continually asking Beth to do it. Every few months Beth fell in love with an abrupt intensity that made Dinah nervous, especially after she had met the current love object and found him, as she always did, an unlikely person for anyone to moon over for hours, usually a young man with gawky limbs and no notion where to put his feet, and once a silent student of art with not a word to say for himself who fell desperately in love with Dinah at their first meeting and hung around for weeks until she managed to convince him she was five years too old for him. Beth had been crazy about him, it had made trouble between the sisters for a while until Beth fell for someone else, and even now she was reluctant to bring her latest guy home in case he flipped over Dinah.

'I'm going to take a shower and change,' Dinah said walking back to the door and Beth looked up.

'Going out?'

'To Mark's party.'

Beth looked interested. 'A party? Can I come? I've never met Mark for more than a minute or two, I'd like a chance to talk to him. Who knows—I may want to go into television when I've left university.'

'What about Garry?' Dinah protested. 'Aren't you seeing him tonight?' She hadn't yet met Beth's latest love; her sister had been very secretive about him, she barely mentioned him except to say that he was a young lecturer in the English department and had black eyes and beautiful hands. Dinah hadn't questioned her closely, she valued her own privacy and did not want to invade her sister's.

'Gary,' Beth corrected. 'And it's finished, over, he's been seeing one of the other girls on the sly.'

'Oh, I'm sorry,' Dinah said uncertainly, noting the feverish look in her sister's amber eyes. How much had Gary mattered to Beth?

'I'll survive,' Beth said through gritted teeth. 'Can I come to the party?' She threw Dinah an appealing look. 'I'll behave angelically, promise.'

Dinah was far from sure how Mark would feel when she appeared with her sister in tow, but he usually said that she could bring a friend if she liked—he meant a man, of course, but Dinah had never taken anyone since she split with Max.

'Well, I don't suppose Mark would mind,' she began and her sister got up and hugged her.

'You're a darling, thanks, I need some cheering up.' She turned away and began to clear the table. 'I'll tidy up in here,' she said, her body skinny in the tight jeans and sweatshirt she was wearing. Beth's figure was boyish, her breasts small, her hips narrow. She had very few clothes, all of them cheap and hard-wearing; in her jeans and dungarees, with her vivid hair cut short, barely reaching her ears and tapering into her nape, she could easily pass for a boy from behind, but she had the fluctuating moods and volatile emotions of a woman, a very young one eager for experience, hungry for life. Dinah sometimes envied her that spontaneous and unashamed vitality; she also worried about her, too, remembering her own deep hurt when she realised why Max had pursued her. Beth was too intense, too open to getting hurt.

While she was showering away the staleness of that hot day Dinah thought about the first programme in her new series. Adam Stuart would be a fascinating subject, it had amazed her when he agreed to do the interview. His reputation was of a man who hated the media, probably because he had suffered at their hands during the early stages of his career. In a sense he exemplified the theme of her series; he had been born in the slums of the East End, illegitimate, abandoned by his mother as a baby and brought up in a children's home from which he had run away at intervals, later fostered by a succession of local women with the same result until he was old enough to get a poorly paid job working on a market stall in Mile End.

Now he was one of the highest paid actors in the film world and the leap between those two vastly different worlds was what Dinah wanted to concentrate on during the interview.

She stepped out of the shower and dried herself, wondering if she was going to find him a difficult man in person. She had stressed the theme of the programme when she talked to the publicity firm who had set up the interview with him; he must know what sort of questions she was going to ask, and be prepared for a certain amount of probing into his childhood background and what effect it had had on him, but with his reputation Dinah would not be amazed if he got angry when she asked personal questions. Apparently one reporter who asked him about his mother had been punched in the face. Dinah hoped he wouldn't get that angry with her. It was a risk she would have to take, she would tread carefully for the first half hour until she had sussed him out.

Beth tapped on the door. 'Hey, have you gone to sleep in the bath? Hurry up, I have to get ready too, remember.'

Dinah wrapped herself in a towelling robe and opened the bathroom door. 'I hope the kitchen is tidy,' she said warningly and Beth made a face at her, slipping past.

'Nag, nag, nag.' She closed the bathroom door and bolted it as her sister made a mock threatening dive back towards her. Through the door Beth yelled: 'I left it as clean as a whistle, so there!'

Dinah went into her bedroom and took off the robe, staring at herself in the mirror with wry appraisal. Her hair was damply curling around her face, the auburn shade darkened by water, her naked body seemed to her to lack any real sex appeal, she was too slim, her breasts high and small, her body long and flat below them, even her hips showing the very faintest curve. She would have liked much richer curves, a body which was magnetic and alluring, full-breasted and rounded in the right places. What happened to her when she met Max had left her with a sense of personal uncertainty; a reluctance to expose herself to that humiliation again, not believing that any man could really want her that much. Her self-confidence at work was in direct ratio to her lack of confidence in her personal life; the less certain of her sexual appeal she became the more she put into her career. At least she could feel that she was in control there; she could assess her success calmly and surely and nobody could fool her.

By the time Beth had had her bath and dressed, Dinah was in the kitchen eating a herb omelette and grilled tomatoes. Beth sauntered in casually and Dinah looked up then did a stunned double take, whistling.

'Like it?' Beth asked, with a satisfied grin. She swivelled so that her sister could admire the full effect of the backless, glittery garment which fell from a very low neckline in a gold-striped waterfall of black pleats to just below her knees. It was very sophisticated, Beth looked years older in it, the gaudy glare of her hair doused by the black material, and a great deal of her smooth pale skin on show.

'You certainly won't be missed in it,' Dinah said, sipping some coffee. There wouldn't be much chance of Beth mingling with the crowd

without Mark noticing her when she looked like
that, and Dinah wondered if it had been
altogether wise of her to say Beth could come.
Some of the Metro crowd—the male members of
it—were likely to be taken in by Beth's outward
sophistication and lively manner. Dinah hoped
there wouldn't be any repercussions from this
party.

Beth was observing her, head to one side. 'You
look cool,' she decided with an approving nod.

'Thank you,' Dinah said, clearing the table.
She did not want to get up in the morning to find
the kitchen in a muddle, and unlike Beth she had
not gone to great pains to make herself look
spectacular. She had put on a white silk sheath
dress with a thin plaited gold belt and blowdried
her hair until it curled softly around her oval
face. The dress wasn't new, she had worn it to
one of Mark's parties not long ago. She was going
tonight because Mark expected it, but she didn't
imagine she would get much fun out of it, she
knew all his guests too well and saw too much of
them around the studios to feel any thrill about
meeting them at a party.

Mark lived in a detached house with gardens
running down to the river in a quiet and
exclusive area west of London but beyond the
urban sprawl. Dinah and Beth took the train out
there but there were always other guests with cars
who would bring them back when the party
ended. Late at night it was sometimes risky
taking public transport, when it was available;
after midnight it had usually stopped running
anyway.

They took a taxi from the station for the last mile. The drive up to Mark's house was crammed with parked cars, the taxi dropped them at the gate and they walked up, hearing other cars arriving and parking in the road. The air was warm, the trees alive with moths which fluttered by them in the purple dusk. A few sleepy birds called with piercing poignancy as though reluctant to go to sleep. A silver crescent moon hung horned and glittering above the black outlines of the trees and Dinah walked slowly, watching it, unwilling to go into the brilliantly lit house to where people talked and laughed and drank while music surged below their voices.

'Come on,' Beth urged impatiently, pulling at her, apparently oblivious of the beauty of the summer night.

'It's beautiful out here,' Dinah murmured, still lingering. 'Very warm for early June; I hope the weather doesn't change again. We could do with a good summer for once.'

Footsteps grated on the gravel of the drive and Beth glanced back curiously as they neared the lamps lighting the front door of the mock Tudor house, illuminating the magpie colours of the façade, black and white, the diamond-paned windows and red-tiled roof. Dinah saw her sister's face brighten. '*Who* is that?' hissed Beth and Dinah looked over her shoulder, half guessing who she would see. Mid-stride, Quinn said: 'Are you waiting for me?' and Dinah's nerves jerked with exasperation at the familiar mockery in that deep voice.

'We weren't, but we are now,' Beth said with

smiling enjoyment, halting, in spite of the fact that Dinah was now in a hurry to get into the house. Quinn drew level with them and Beth held out a hand. 'Hi! I'm a gatecrasher, I twisted Dinah's arm to make her bring me, I'm her sister, Beth.'

'Hallo,' he said, not releasing her hand and staring at her with unhidden curiosity. 'I'm Quinn Howard, I work at Metro.' In the dusky shadows Dinah clearly saw the slow rise of his fine black brows as he took in Beth's glittering sophistication and her lively smile. 'Where do you work?' he asked and Beth groaned.

'I wish you hadn't asked that! I'm a student, doing modern languages. . . .'

Dinah moved ahead into the house and heard her sister's voice going on behind her, Quinn's curious questions interrupting now and then. Why had it been Quinn Howard they ran into so early in the evening? Dinah had hoped to keep him and Beth apart as long as she could, she didn't want her sister getting tangled up with a guy like him, although Beth was probably in no danger from Quinn since she had nothing he wanted. Beth couldn't further those consuming ambitions of his. Dinah's frown deepened as she said hallo to Mark in the hall, and slid out of her jacket. Quinn might chase Beth for other reasons, of course; her sister was sexually vital and he was a man who was very aware of the other sex.

'Why the scowl?' Mark asked, watching her, then his gaze flicked to the doorway as Quinn and Beth walked into the house. Mark looked amused. 'Now I wonder where he found her?

She's a sexy little item.' He stopped short, his eyes narrowing. 'That isn't your sister?' He looked down at Dinah, his mouth wry. 'It is, isn't it? I didn't recognise her for a minute. She looks a damned sight more grown up than she did last time I met her. I always think of her as a teenager. I must be getting old.'

'Don't let her fool you—she's only twenty,' Dinah said, but very softly, so that Beth shouldn't hear her and be enraged. 'I hope you don't mind me bringing her, she just lost her latest boyfriend and she was feeling very down, I thought it might cheer her up to come with me.'

'She's welcome,' Mark said, grinning. 'Anything that decorative is always welcome at my parties.' He had pitched his voice so that Beth heard him and her eyes flashed across to his, her face alight.

'Hallo, Mark—it's ages since I saw you. How are you?' Beth sounded very adult, the swaying movement of her body in the low-cut dress even more so, and Dinah crossed her fingers behind her back as she watched Beth stand on tiptoe to kiss Mark's cheek. Beth was behaving very recklessly tonight; it was worrying.

'You look gorgeous,' Mark said, holding her slender waist with both hands and gently pushing her away. 'Go and find a drink, all of you, while I do my duty and behave like a host.' His voice was friendly yet had a delicately distancing note; Dinah knew she need not be afraid that Mark would take advantage of Beth's extrovert behaviour, he had picked up her warning when she told him Beth was only twenty. Mark was a man who liked women but was not a womaniser. If he was lonely since he lost his wife he seemed to accept it. Plenty of women at Metro would jump at a chance to date him but he seemed blind to their interest in him.

Dinah drifted into the crowded party, picking up a glass of gin and orange en route, and was greeted at once by a small group avidly discussing some gossip about one of the current affairs producers who was reputed to be having an affair with his secretary. Dinah knew the man's wife and soon moved away, her mouth distasteful. She hoped it wasn't true, such rumours often fizzled out, based on nothing more circumstantial than an overheard remark or a chance glance between the suspected pair. Dinah certainly wasn't wasting her time talking about it, true or otherwise.

She looked back in search of Beth; hoping she was not with Quinn Howard. You don't leave a child alone with dynamite, and in spite of Beth's twenty years there was still a lot of the child in her, especially where her passion for experiment was concerned.

Dinah saw her almost at once, in a semi-circle of men arranged facing her like the petals fanning out from the heart of a daisy, they were all laughing and Beth was looking pleased with herself. Dinah watched wryly; well, there was safety in numbers, Beth couldn't come to any harm with that many men to choose from. It was Quinn Howard who made Dinah's blood run cold, he was far too sophisticated for Beth, for all her finery tonight. Beth's sophistication was borrowed, a purely surface gloss; Dinah knew that Quinn Howard's was the real thing which made him a man to steer clear of.

'Hallo, Dinah,' John Mower said, putting a hand over her arm to attract her attention. 'Have you met my wife? Ann, this is Dinah Sheraton.'

'How nice to meet you at last, I haven't missed any of your programmes, they're always so good.' His wife was a surprise, a warm and bouncy woman with untidy curls and very bright, shiny blue eyes. She was plump and rather short and wore a vaguely oriental garment which came close to being a sari; it was draped across her large bosom in loose folds and fell to her feet, the enormous tropical flowers printed on the material so staggering that they made you forget everything else as you stared at them. Dinah couldn't take her eyes off their unreal colour while Ann Mower talked at her, not waiting for any replies, just chattering at random about the station, the programmes, the people who ran them. Dinah noticed with some irony that, having pushed his wife at her, John Mower had slipped away.

When Ann Mower did stop talking Dinah didn't realise it for a second, then focused on her hurriedly, wondering if she had actually asked a question to which she wanted a reply. The other woman wasn't looking at her, though; she was staring at the man who had just loomed up beside them. Dinah saw the sheen of excitement and avid curiosity in Ann Mower's rounded eyes and looked up into Quinn's face, on a reflex action, her mouth compressing.

'Enjoying the party?' Quinn divided the

question between them, smiling at Ann Mower but managing to give Dinah a mocking glance at the same time which made her wonder if he had been watching her and the other woman in their one-sided conversation.

'We haven't met, have we?' Ann Mower told him, holding out her hand. 'I'm Ann Mower.'

Quinn said he knew, he was glad to know her. 'What a striking dress,' he said, overdoing the admiring look over it, in Dinah's opinion, but Ann seemed delighted, she beamed from ear to ear and said she had made it herself.

'How clever of you,' Quinn said and Dinah looked away, trying not to laugh; it wasn't fair, poor woman, and the fact that she was obviously very pleased with her dress didn't make it any the less unkind of Quinn to make fun of her. Dinah looked back at him and could see no hint of humour in his face, he seemed perfectly serious as he asked if Ann Mower had used a pattern or designed the dress herself, and Ann was certainly serious as she answered.

'I never get a chance to meet the people John works with,' Ann said. 'I've been looking forward to this party for weeks.' She looked around the room, sighing, a hectic flush on her cheeks and her eyes eager. 'Seeing you all on the box and then actually seeing you in the flesh,' she said vaguely. 'Isn't it funny how you feel you know people you see on television? I mean, every night you come into our sitting rooms, just like one of the family, really, but we don't actually know you.'

'Odd feeling, isn't it?' Quinn said and Dinah

looked at him in surprise and thought; he's being very kind to her, there was no sign of the irony and mockery he always aimed at *her*. He was apparently taking Ann Mower as seriously as she took herself and when he smiled at the other woman his eyes were almost gentle; that was an expression Dinah had never seen in those cool blue eyes.

'It is,' Ann Mower said, still staring around.

'Tell me who you'd like to meet and I'll introduce you,' Quinn offered and Ann gave a happy little sigh like someone offered a very special present they've yearned for for years.

'Well,' she said, dithering between one face and another, then she frowned. 'I don't know *him*, although I feel I ought to, his face is very familiar. Is he an actor? I think that's where I've seen him before.'

Dinah had casually glanced in the direction Ann's eyes had taken, then she had stiffened from head to foot in deadly shock as she recognised the man talking to Mark near the door. She hadn't seen him for two years except in advertisements and once in a play which she had begun to watch without realising he was in it and which she had switched off hurriedly as soon as she saw his face. He had changed more than she had expected; after all, two years isn't a long time and she wouldn't have thought it would do much more than give him a deeper gloss of self-confidence. Success usually does. Max had undoubtedly altered, though; he was far more casual, relaxed, as he talked to Mark he wasn't putting out all his charm the way he had when she knew him. She got the feeling Max no longer felt he needed to work so hard to impress people, he could do that now without lifting a finger, and his body radiated a lazy assurance. He had made it, that lounging posture said, indifferent now to the eyes which might be watching him. He expected that, he discounted it.

'That's Max Tracy,' Quinn had said, smiling, and Ann had babbled amazement and excitement while Dinah was staring, her face rigid. Quinn glanced at her and his brows met. Dinah felt his stare and quickly looked away from Max at another part of the room, searching now for her sister. Beth was still ringed by men and having a great time judging by her laughter. She was holding a glass but while Dinah watched Beth didn't drink any of the red wine in it; she wasn't getting her euphoria by the glass, anyway. She was high on the fun of being admired and Dinah relaxed, looking round at Quinn and Ann Mower again.

'Did you see him in that spy series? Wasn't he marvellous? It was a small part in the beginning but he was so good they kept building the part up.'

'He's been the find of the year, it seems,' Quinn said, watching Dinah. 'I can't take you over to meet him, I don't know him, I'm afraid. We could join Mark and ask him to introduce you, though.'

Mark had taken Max over to meet some of the other guests and left him with them, Dinah saw with a swift, secret look.

'You don't know him, do you, Dinah?' Quinn

asked and she gave him a startled look, eyes wide and nervous.

'I'm not in drama,' she said evasively. 'Actors don't come into my programmes, although I am going to be interviewing Adam Stuart in a few weeks' time.'

'Oh, are you? You lucky girl,' Ann Mower said ecstatically. 'Did you see him in that last film? I was on the edge of my seat, it was nerve-wracking. He acts without you noticing, if you know what I mean.'

'He's very natural,' Dinah agreed, launching deliberately into a discussion of Adam Stuart because it was safer than allowing Quinn to ask any of the questions about Max that she sensed hovering on his tongue. He was too perceptive; how had he picked up the vibrations inside her when she first saw Max? Had her face given her away? She must watch that, get a tight hold on herself. What was Max doing here? Had Mark invited him or had someone brought him?—and if so, who? Mark's parties were always crowded with people from television and the rest of the media, anyone might have asked Max to come with them.

'I suppose you couldn't get me Adam Stuart's autograph?' Ann Mower said wistfully and Dinah laughed and said she would try, if she got the chance, and no, she wouldn't forget, she promised.

'He's difficult, though; I'll wait and see how I get on with him,' she said and Mark joined them, smiling, a glass of whisky in his hand.

'Who's difficult? Not me, I hope?'

Ann Mower laughed and Mark smiled at her with faint surprise. 'You haven't got a drink, can I get you one? John should have made sure you weren't left empty-handed, we can't have that.' He sounded as though he knew her well and Ann looked delighted, shaking her head.

'I've had enough to drink, thank you; I find it makes my head ache next day.'

'You and me both,' Mark said, drinking half the whisky in one swallow.

'Was that Max Tracy we just saw you with?' Ann asked, pushing back a wandering tendril of hair from her pink face, and Mark agreed that it had been, he had come along with some people from the drama department.

'He's going to do a play for us,' he added with satisfaction. 'We snatched him up before the crowd got in; this time next year he'll probably be very hard to get. He's going to be one of the big names, that's obvious.' Swirling the whisky in his glass while he watched it, he added wryly: 'He deserves it, he's worked hard enough for it, but then you have to be ruthless to get anywhere in that dog eat dog world.' He looked at Dinah and she looked away, aware that she was pale. Her skin felt cold and tight across her cheekbones, as though her face had shrunk. Mark knew, she had forgotten that; they had never talked about it, Mark was far too tactful to bring up a subject he felt might be painful, but he remembered, his eyes told her that. They questioned her; had she got over Max? Was he a burnt-out ember?

'I'd love to meet him,' Ann angled pleadingly and Mark looked around, frowning.

'He's over there,' he said after a pause while he searched the room for Max, and Dinah involuntarily looked past the chattering little groups of people and with a stab of alarm saw Max in a corner, propping himself lazily with one hand on the wall, while he bent his blond head down towards Beth, watching her with amused, appreciative eyes.

'She's pretty,' Ann said thoughtfully, laughing. 'Well, we'd better not interrupt him just now, he looks too absorbed in *her*.'

He did, he wasn't taking his eyes from Beth's glowing, lively face and she was gazing back at him, sparkling like a Christmas tree. Dinah's heart plunged.

'Excuse me,' she muttered and walked towards them, forgetting everything but a fierce refusal to watch her sister suffer as she had at the hands of Max Tracy. Beth was on the rebound at the moment, looking for something that would soothe her wounded pride after her latest young man had let her down. She wouldn't see beneath the surface of Max's charm; she wouldn't want to. He was good looking, he was rapidly becoming a well-known name, his interest in Beth would be too flattering to resist. Dinah walked quickly, her memory besieged by the past, remembering all too vividly how bowled over she had been when she was on the receiving end of Max's heart-stopping smile. She hadn't believed her luck, either. She could easily imagine how her sister felt.

Max lazily lifted his head and Dinah halted in front of them, smiling too brightly, her lips drawn back from her teeth in a frozen grimace she tried to make more convincing.

'Dinah!' he said on a deep, warm note, and swung to hold out his hands. She had to put her own into them and Max held them, staring down at her as if doing some remembering of his own, while Beth watched with a surprised expression.

'You look marvellous!' he said, lying in his teeth.

'So do you,' Dinah said with the same sincerity, but her vivid eyes blazed with contempt she half-veiled by her lashes, carefully staying in profile to her sister so that Beth shouldn't see it, but not hiding it from Max.

'You've been holding out on me,' Beth accused. 'You never said you knew Max!'

'Didn't I? Oh, well, I've met so many public faces, it's hard to remember them all,' Dinah said in a pretence of casual amusement her eyes did not echo, and Max laughed wryly.

'Had you forgotten me? There's a knock for my ego!'

It could do with one, Dinah's eyes told him, and he tightened his grip on her hands which he still held and drew her towards him. She knew what he was going to do before he did it and she could have pulled away but she didn't, not with Beth watching them. She even lifted her face, offered him her mouth, as casually as she had kissed several of the wives of men she had worked with for years; kissing meant little in their world, she wasn't going to make a big scene over a kiss from Max. It might burn her mouth like acid but she was going to be a spartan and refuse to show a thing.

He brushed his mouth over hers softly; she knew he must be aware of her resistance even though she allowed the kiss, her whole body was tense, rejecting him, but when Max drew away she saw the light, gleaming brightness of his eyes. They were restless eyes, those of a man always looking somewhere else for new heights to conquer, they were shallow and vain, lacking depth. Why hadn't she seen that before? How had he ever managed to make her believe he could make any woman happy? He couldn't give happiness because he didn't have it in himself; he had nothing to give, he was consumed with a selfish desire to take, whatever life offered Max wanted, but he would give nothing back.

Mark had wandered over, watching as they drew apart, his brows quizzical as Dinah looked at him. He had the expression of someone watching children misbehave, his eyes ironic, asking if she knew what she was doing. 'They're dancing in the other room now,' he said, then turned to Beth, holding out a hand. 'Come and show me how to do it, I've forgotten.'

Beth was looking aggrieved; she had found Max first and had been getting on fine with him until Dinah came along and broke it up. She hadn't had a clue that Dinah knew him but that kiss had made it clear they knew each other better than casual acquaintances and Beth was sulky, but her eyes brightened as she looked at Mark. He was rather too old for her, of course, but he was famous, an important guy in television with charisma and status. Beth had hoped to get a chance to talk to him sometime.

'Okay, come on, then,' she said. 'See you,' she added to the other two.

Max hadn't taken his eyes off Dinah; her coldness when he kissed her had been a challenge, there was a flare of interest in his shallow eyes. He half smiled in Beth's direction, nodding. 'See you,' he said and when the other two had gone he said to Dinah: 'It's too noisy in here, we've got a lot of catching up to do—why don't we go into the garden? It's a wonderful night, very warm out there. A pity to waste that moonlight.'

'We haven't got anything to talk about,' Dinah said with a contemptuous smile. 'There are plenty of important people here, people with influence—let me introduce you to some. They can help you more than I can now.'

'I don't want to talk to anyone else—I came to talk to you,' he said. 'That's the only reason I'm here. When someone said Mark was having a party, did I want to go along, I thought: I wonder if Dinah will be there? I suddenly realised I wanted to see you again. We should never have lost touch, but then we've both been busy building our careers, haven't we? I always knew you were going to the top, you know, you were always clever.' He gave her that charming smile she no longer found convincing and she stared at him speechlessly, hardly believing her ears.

Did he really believe all that? Perhaps he did. Max lived in a world of illusion where seeming became being and emotion was one-dimensional; put on with his make-up and sloughed like an outworn skin once it was no longer needed. He was tinsel and stardust and by the bleak light of reality Dinah saw the tawdry nature of his charm with clarity, almost sorry for him, but even more pitying herself as she had been three years ago, a wide-eyed little fool who couldn't see further than the end of her nose.

'You were too clever for me,' Max said. 'You could always run rings around me, I wasn't surprised when your programmes started getting awards.'

Dinah's temper rose like mercury, she was very flushed as she realised why he was turning that charm on her again. Max was paying homage to her success in television, he thought she might be a useful person to know, he was trying to paper over the past, change the way she saw it as well as the way she saw him.

'I never miss one of your programmes if I can help it,' he said. 'You've climbed the ladder fast, haven't you?'

'Not as fast as you have,' Dinah said fiercely, leaning towards him. 'You've shot up and I was the bottom rung on your ladder, wasn't I? You stepped on my face on your way up and that isn't something anyone forgets.'

Max had gone red; he looked around them in agitation as people turned to stare and whisper. Dinah could have kicked herself, she hadn't meant to erupt like that, it had burst out of her. She turned to walk away and tried to look unconcerned as she got curious looks. Quinn was

on the far side of the room, he couldn't have
heard what she said but she felt his blue eyes
watching her although she didn't meet that stare.
She pushed her way through a crowd of people,
and went to look for Beth among the dancing
couples in the other room. Her sister was still
with Mark; they were both laughing helplessly as
Mark tried to imitate Beth's gyrations with little
success.

'Don't be so self-conscious! You're too inhib-
ited!' Beth told him, then slid her arms round his
neck and snuggled against him. 'Look, forget the
other stuff—we'll do it the old-fashioned way.'

Mark grinned, holding her by the waist with
both hands. 'Now you're talking! This I can do.'

Dinah left them to it; Beth would be safe
enough with Mark. She went into the kitchen and
got herself a glass of water, dropped a few pieces
of ice into it and swirled it around, clinking,
while she tried to cool down. Her face was far too
hot and her pulse was racing, the adrenalin of
rage still running through her.

She went out into the garden through the back
door from the kitchen and wandered along the
narrow crazy-paving paths between flowerbeds
and under trees, her way picked out by treacherous
moonlight. Mark had a large garden, laid out in
formal geometric patterns, a diamond of green
lawn edged by strips of flower beds here, a circle of
rose trees enclosing a paved area there, a square
vegetable garden with box tree hedges right at the
far end of it, and behind a line of rhododendron
bushes a large goldfish pond which had a low
concrete wall running all round it.

Dinah sat down on the top of the wall, breathing more calmly now; she dabbled her fingers in the cool water and splashed some on her hot face. Delicious, she thought, half closing her eyes. She could hear the noise of the party at a distance but she felt insulated from it out here, the edges of the garden crowded with the dark shadows of trees motionless in the still summer night.

She sipped her drink for a while, watching the surface of the water; it was thick with dark green waxen leaves and white flowers folded for the night, not an inch between them, no room for the moon to see its face. A goldfish slipped past her finger, making her flesh prickle, and she bent her head to peer into the water, pushing aside the waterlilies and their cool leaves. All she saw was her own face, dimly wavering, and then another face appeared behind hers and Dinah stared at it, stupefied. She hadn't heard anyone coming.

Her head swung round and Quinn Howard looked at her with a searching frown. 'What are you doing out here?'

She had recovered from the first shock of seeing him, she shrugged, picking up her glass and sipping more water. 'I was hot.'

'You weren't running away from Tracy, then?' he asked, his tone sarcastic now.

'No, I wasn't,' Dinah said, reddening. 'Why should I?'

'I was going to ask you that.'

'Well, I asked first,' she said, putting down her glass because the temptation to fling its contents into his face might prove too great if she went on holding it much longer.

'Do I gather you used to see a lot of him at one time?' he asked slowly, picking his words with obvious care.

'I don't know what you gather. I was enjoying the peace and quiet out here, why don't you go back to the party?'

'Why don't you?' he simply asked drily. 'Afraid of hearing what people are whispering about you and Tracy?'

She fizzed with rage, eyeing him with a yearning little short of homicidal intention. 'You can't stop needling me, can you? Every time I see you, you try to get under my skin.' He watched her without answering, his face ironic in the moonlight, which carved deep hollows along his cheekbones and made his eyes glitter. 'You don't deny it, I notice!' Dinah said with angry satisfaction in this mute admission.

He leaned towards her, holding her gaze, and she had a sudden shaken suspicion that he was going to kiss her. Her body involuntarily shrank backwards and the next second she realised she was toppling into the pond. She gave a strangled yelp, reaching for him, her fingers clutching his shirt. Quinn made an odd little noise, somewhere between an exclamation and a laugh, grabbing at her with both hands, but it was too late. Dinah fell into the water with a loud splash, and sank like a stone.

CHAPTER THREE

SHE fought her way back to the surface, spluttering as water ran into her open mouth, not realising she was yelling. Kicking and struggling, she wasn't aware of anything but the need to get out of the water. She could only have been in the pond for a few seconds, but it seemed like eternity at the time; then Quinn leaned over and took hold of her shoulders and dragged her, dripping, across the wall. Sagging, she coughed and gasped for air. He slapped her on the back and she protested angrily, but inaudibly. Quinn bent over her, still massaging her back.

'What did you say?'

Dinah shook her head to clear the water out of her ears, ran her hands down her streaming face to make sure she could see him and glared at him. 'I said don't *do* that!'

'What?' he asked, apparently baffled.

'Hit me on the back! Do you want me to throw up?'

'No,' he agreed hurriedly, retreating. 'Are you going to?'

She looked at him with a vengeful eye. 'I'm considering it.' Water was pouring from her saturated dress which clung to her body like a second skin. Dinah didn't know whether to scream or burst into tears so she compromised and yelled at Quinn angrily. 'Look at me! How am I going to get home like this? I can't go back into the party in this state but I can't wander about dripping until I can get home and change. This is all your fault, you pushed me, I felt you do it, you ... you. ...' Epithets failed her. She stammered into a breathless silence and it was then that Quinn laughed.

Dinah couldn't believe her ears, she stared at him in total disbelief. He was staring at her, too, and the more he looked the more he laughed.

'What's funny?'

'You'd know if you could see yourself,' he said. 'You're absolutely sodden.'

'I had noticed,' Dinah said, vibrating with rage.

'You look like a drowned rat.'

Her teeth met and she shifted her feet in the pool of water which had formed around her. 'I've lost my damned shoes,' she said, only realising it at that moment. She looked around the crazy paving, there was no sign of them. Quinn hunted briefly then glanced into the pond, his amusement coming back. 'They're in there, I'm afraid,' he said, audibly stifling more laughter.

'Yes,' Dinah said flintily.

'You'd better go upstairs, have a shower and get into a dressing-gown or something,' he thought aloud.

'Mark isn't going to like me dripping up his stairs.'

'It wasn't your fault you fell into his pond.'

'I know whose fault it was,' Dinah said and his dangerously intelligent blue eyes mocked her wickedly.

'I did not push you, I tried to grab you but you slipped out of my hands.' He smiled oddly. 'As usual,' he added, but Dinah didn't register that until later.

'I was trying to get my balance,' she said.

'And now you're very wet,' he said coolly. 'And if you aren't to get pneumonia I think you should get out of those clothes right away. It may be a warm night but you can still catch a chill.'

He took her elbow to propel her towards the house and Dinah bristled at being hustled around by a man she didn't like. She pulled her arm free. 'I'm not walking through the party like this! If you'll call me a taxi I'll go straight home.'

'I'll drive you,' he said. 'But first you must have a warm bath and put on some dry clothes. You can't drive about in wet clothes. If we go up the back stairs, nobody will see you.' He pushed open a side door of the house. 'In here and up those stairs,' he ordered and Dinah peered up from the gloomy little corridor. 'This was the servants' staircase,' Quinn told her. 'Big houses always used to have them so that the housemaids could go up and down stairs without their employers seeing them.'

Dinah hesitated. 'Hadn't we better ask Mark's permission first?'

'We'll tell him later, I'll go down and explain while you're having a bath.' He urged her with a hand in the small of her back. 'Go on!'

She obeyed, grim faced; the stairs were narrow and uncarpeted, looking back she saw her own wet footprints following them on the wooden treads. She was shivering now, her clothes dripping everywhere she went. Quinn gestured towards a door on the landing they reached.

'Through here.' The stairs wound up further towards the attics and Dinah glanced at them. Quinn followed her eyes. 'The servants used to sleep up there,' he explained. 'Having their private staircase meant that they could get up at crack of dawn and slip silently down to the kitchen to start work while the gentry lay in bed until the breakfast gong. A nice life.'

'Lovely,' Dinah said bitterly. 'I know where I'd have been—up in the attic.' She trudged damply through the door and found herself in a thickly carpeted corridor. The sound of the party was more audible up there, she heard music and laughter much closer.

Quinn opened another door. 'I think this is . . . yes, it's the bathroom.' He walked into it and Dinah stood on the threshold, fulminating.

'I'm not taking a bath with you watching me, what are you doing in there? I don't need any help, thank you, you can get out of here right now.'

When her angry voice paused he said mildly: 'I was looking to see if there were clean towels and there are—there's a robe on the back of the door, too, you can put that on when you've had your bath. I'll go down and tell Mark what's happened. What size are you?' He went over to the bath and began running hot water.

'What?' Dinah was confused. Did he intend to stay here while she had this bath?

'You aren't all *that* large,' he murmured thoughtfully staring at her, and she almost hissed.

'I am not large at all. I'm a size ten, if that's what you mean.'

'Mark's son may have some jeans that will fit you, or you could wear one of Mark's sweaters as a dress.'

'Merciful heavens,' Dinah breathed. 'Get out.'

'Just a suggestion,' he said, walking past her, smiling.

'And you can tell Mark that his pond is too deep, I could have drowned.' Dinah slammed the door, bolted it and began to pull off her clothes, halting for a second as she caught sight of her reflection in the large wall mirror. Hot colour ran into her face. My God, her clothes were completely transparent, the white silk had moulded itself to her body so tightly that she might as well be wearing nothing, you could see her panties and bra, the rounded flesh of her breasts and the flat midriff beneath them, the soft curve of her belly and hips, the dark triangle of hair between her thighs. It hadn't occurred to her while Quinn was staring at her a moment ago that he was seeing her as clearly as if she was naked.

It bothered her. It would have bothered her whoever had seen her but that it should be Quinn left her feeling disturbed especially as those blue eyes hadn't betrayed what they were seeing, she had been more concerned with looking ridiculous than with any idea that he was staring at her nude body. She dragged off her clothes and dropped them into the washbasin in a clammy huddle, poured some pine-scented bathsalts, from a glass jar, into the bath, and swished the cloudy water until they had dissolved, then climbed gratefully into that perfumed warmth.

Her body was all gooseflesh, she was almost blue with cold, her teeth chattering. For a few moments she just lay there, up to her neck in water, letting the warmth permeate her until she had stopped shuddering. Eyes closed she wondered what had really been going on inside Quinn's head while he studied her a while ago; she had known those blue eyes held curiosity and an intent attention but she hadn't picked up any sexual awareness. Maybe there had been none to pick up. She couldn't have looked desirable.

The water was too hot, she decided, feeling the heat in her face and body. She sat up, banishing thoughts of Quinn Howard. She didn't want him to desire her, anyway, she told herself impatiently. She unhooked the shower fitment and began to wash her hair, rinsing away the weedy water from the pond and a scrap of green leaf which had become embedded among the damp strands.

Ten minutes later she got out of the bath, towelled herself vigorously with one of the large, lemon bathtowels which had been chosen to match the yellow bath and contrast with the pale green tiles on the walls, and then put on the white robe hanging on the door. It was much too large, she had to roll up the sleeves and the hem almost came down to her ankles. She looked absurd in it, but it was clean and dry.

She opened the door, wondering how much longer Quinn would be, and found him leaning against the wall outside, his arms folded and a patient look on his face. He straightened, smiling.

'Mark sends his apologies for his pond, he's relieved you didn't drown and you're to feel free to wear anything of his that fits. His is the bedroom on the right; he said you can rummage for clothes yourself.' He moved lazily, his hand lifted to her hair and Dinah stiffened, but he was only pulling the hood of the robe over her head. 'Now you look like a nun,' he told her, laughing.

'I don't know why you seem to find this so funny. I don't.' Her skin was bristling with an antagonism which was almost physical; as though her body reacted to his presence the way it reacted to certain pollens to which she was allergic. For a week or two each year she couldn't stop sneezing, she came out in a rash, she had red eyes and a sore throat until whichever grass it was she could not tolerate had stopped seeding. Her response to Quinn Howard was of the same instinctive, inexplicable order.

'Your sense of humour has always been suspect,' Quinn said with dry impatience.

'Why don't you go back to the party?' Dinah merely retorted. 'I'll find some clothes and ring for a taxi.'

'I'll take you home.'

'You won't,' she said, her mouth tight, and his blue eyes narrowed on her, bright with awareness, but of what? she wondered, knowing she had flushed. Hurriedly she asked: 'Is Beth okay? Did you see her? Is she with Mark?'

Quinn considered her, his fine black brows arched. 'She seems to be having a wonderful time, she was dancing with Mark.' He watched the relief she couldn't hide as it filled her eyes.

'What were you afraid she might be doing?' he asked.

She turned away, her nerves jumping. 'I'd better find some clothes.' She padded towards Mark's bedroom with Quinn prowling behind her. The back of Dinah's neck prickled as though his soft tread was that of a predator on her trail. 'Where are you going?' she asked aggressively.

'Mark told me where to find his sweaters.' Quinn walked across the room while Dinah hesitated near the door, staring around the bedroom curiously. It was spacious and high-ceilinged, decorated in shades of blue and white; with striped brocade curtains and silky wallpaper, a pale blue carpet and in the very centre of the room a vast, king-sized bed with a dark blue cover and a pleated valance in the same colour falling to the carpet. Everything in the room was immaculately tidy; Mark's housekeeper was obviously painstaking or as afraid of Mark as everyone who worked at Metro.

Quinn had opened a door in the long, fitted wardrobe whose white doors held full-sized mirrors which flashed as Quinn pushed them open. He selected a dark green V-necked pullover from the neat pile stacked in one deep compartment, tossed it to her, saying: 'Try that.'

She held it against her protectively. 'When you've gone,' she said pointedly.

Making no comment on that, Quinn flicked through a row of shirts hanging in another part of the wardrobe. He pulled down a closely tailored white one and held it out, walking towards her.

Dinah took it, backing immediately. Quinn's

smile had gone, he was frowning blackly. 'I'm
sick of having you look at me as if I was Jack the
Ripper,' he said angrily and Dinah took another
step away only to find the back of her knees
against the bed, but too late to save herself from
losing her balance. She sprawled backwards with
a frantic yelp, landing on the bed with Quinn
kneeling over her.

'What do you think you're doing?' Dinah said
breathlessly as she realised she couldn't get up.
He had anchored her to the bed, his knees
gripping her waist and alarm made her throat
beat with a disturbed pulse.

He took no notice of what she said, staring at
her intently as though he had never seen her
before. She felt the insistent probe of his eyes as
though they were redhot needles inserted under
her skin. Dinah tried to say something else but
her mouth was too dry; the silence dragged
between them inertly while from downstairs she
heard the sound of the party; the noise was
unabated, voices and laughter competing with the
underthrob of music. They were all having a
good time and Dinah felt excluded, shut out,
apart from them, but more than that she felt as
though this silent room was a desert island on
which she and Quinn were the only inhabitants.
She stared up at him, limp now, melancholy
settling on her like fine grey ash from a dead fire
which some sudden wind has blown across a
peaceful landscape, as she wondered if Max had
gone and what he was doing.

'What exactly happened between you and Max
Tracy?' he asked at last and her eyes flickered

angrily, half afraid he might have read her thoughts.

'None of your business,' she muttered, trying to push him away. 'Will you get off me?' He didn't budge and her palms flattened against his shirt; she felt a sharp jab of sexual awareness as she became conscious of the warmth of his lean, muscular chest beneath the thin silk. Quinn's heart was beating heavily, it seemed to be very fast, the crash of it reverberated under her hands.

'You were in love with him,' Quinn stated flatly. Dinah had always found his mockery intolerable but she found his new mood worse. There was something in his eyes which worried her.

'Are you *still* in love with him?' Quinn asked, a trace of harshness in his voice and Dinah went red.

'If someone comes in here they'll think. . . .' she began and his mouth twisted with angry derision.

'I know what they'd think,' he said and his hand moved like a snake. He had untied her belt before she knew what he was doing. Dinah gave a stifled gasp of shock and grabbed for the robe just as Quinn's head swooped down and his hard mouth closed over her own, silencing the wild cry she gave. Her hands were imprisoned between them, she couldn't struggle free, his kiss forced back her head and his hands wandered lingeringly caressing the warm, naked flesh he was holding captive with the weight of his own body. The stroke of his fingertips sent an unexpected wave of sensual pleasure pouring through Dinah; it shocked her, frightened her. The intimate invasion of her mouth, the ache of her stretched throat, were an attack to which she was defenceless, her struggles only seemed to incite him, and the physical reaction of her own body made her frantic to get away before she betrayed herself into his hands.

She began to kick and writhe, heaving her body in an attempt to force him off, and Quinn's head lifted, he stared down at her with eyes dilated with excitement.

'Do I have to scream for help?' Dinah whispered, her throat sore. Quinn was dark red now, she heard him breathing in a harsh, irregular way. He was staring at her body, she saw him half close his eyes, then he swung off the bed and silently walked out of the room, slamming the door behind him.

Dinah staggered off the bed and made it to the door before her legs gave way. She shot the bolt and leaned on the panels, trembling. Her heart was thudding against her ribs, her mouth felt swollen and hot. She didn't know exactly what she felt, torn between rage and incredulity. How close had she come to being raped just now? Was that what had been in his mind?

She shakily walked over to the wardrobe and stared at herself in the long mirrors, her body naked between the open robe. There were red marks on her throat and shoulders where Quinn had gripped her, she saw the prints of his fingertips in her pale flesh, but the other signs he had left on her were less obvious but more disturbing. Her mouth was full and red, moist with heat where he had used it ruthlessly, the faint swelling visible to her if not to everyone else when they saw it. Her breasts were enlarged with blood, the blue veins visible on the smooth skin, her nipples hard and dark red, she felt them aching and bit her lip in dismay. She had not anticipated that abrupt intensity of desire inside herself; she didn't even like Quinn Howard, she didn't want him, but while he was making love to her she *had* wanted him. She turned away angrily, hating the admission but having to face it.

It would be easy enough to reassure herself by saying that Quinn had forced her to submit to him, but that wouldn't explain the aroused state of her body or the dull ache of frustration as her heated blood began to cool.

She put on the white shirt, her fingers so shaky that it took several minutes to get it buttoned. She felt warmer when she had slipped the green sweater over her head and pulled it down; it reached her upper thighs covering most of her, but she didn't fancy the idea of walking through the crowded house like that. She found some of Mark's underpants and a pair of old, well-washed jeans. They were much too big, but she rolled up the hems and used a broad leather belt to make sure they didn't sag too much. Her reflection now was comic; she looked like Charlie Chaplin, the old jeans baggy, the sweater far too long. With an angry shrug she completed the outfit with a pair of Mark's socks; her bare feet were freezing. She tucked the ends of the jeans into the socks and looked at herself again. Anyone who saw her would think she had just escaped from a jumble sale wearing all her purchases.

She took a deep breath, nerving herself to go out and face whoever was around. When she opened the door the party was just as noisy, she looked down the main stairs and saw Quinn's dark head. He was waiting for her. While she hesitated, he looked round, his face shuttered. He was carrying her handbag and jacket, which he handed her, when he came up the stairs. 'We'll go out the way we came in,' he said, his eyes not meeting hers. 'Mark promises to bring Beth home himself.' He looked at her feet. 'You'll need shoes, borrow some of Mark's.'

'They're too big, I can't walk in them.' She was very flushed and breathless.

'You'll have to try,' he said so she doggedly went back into the bedroom and took a pair of casual shoes out of the rack in the wardrobe. She carried them under her arm as they went back down the narrow servants' stairs but before she went out she slid her feet into them. Quinn walked fast, at a loping stride; Dinah followed slowly a few paces behind him, her feet slipping about inside Mark's shoes. She had to walk like some little Japanese lady, taking tiny steps. Quinn had parked out on the road; it took what seemed hours to reach his car and Dinah's calf muscles ached with the strain of trying not to lose one of her shoes.

She collapsed inside Quinn's car with relief. He got in beside her and started the engine without a word. He didn't say anything as he drove her home, either, but when he had parked outside her flat he turned and looked briefly at her. 'I apologise for what happened earlier,' he said in a grim voice as though it was Dinah who was really at fault. She risked a look at him; his features were cold, set, the yellow gleam of the street lighting gave them an ominous hue, half in the light, half out of it, in a harlequin patterning.

She couldn't think of anything to say, she fumbled for the door handle and Quinn spoke again. 'It got out of control.'

'You mean you did,' Dinah muttered, turned away from him.

He gave a rough sigh. 'I can't explain. . . .'

'You don't need to—any woman who works in an office full of men knows it may happen any time; men are sexual opportunists, given the right circumstances they take every chance they can, although I'm damned if I can see what pleasure you get out of forcing yourself on a woman who doesn't want you, I'd find it humiliating. I find it humiliating having had to put up with it. I don't want to talk about it any more, it makes me sick just to remember it.'

She swung her legs out of the car and lost a shoe. Angrily picking it up she limped round on to the pavement and into the building. She heard Quinn drive away with a roar of power, his tyres screeching. Typical male—take his temper out behind a wheel! she thought, hunting for her key. One of her neighbours came up behind her, Dinah looked round in flushed embarrassment and got an incredulous, curious smile. She felt the door give and shot inside her flat before she could be asked any questions.

She would never go to one of Mark's parties again, she told herself, as she got undressed; but that didn't help her solve the main problem bothering her now. How on earth was she going to face Quinn Howard in the office after this?

She was half asleep when Beth came home and slipped quietly into their bedroom. Dinah opened one eye to peer at the clock; it was one o'clock. Beth was tiptoeing about in the shadowy room with only the fugitive light from the streetlamp outside to guide her. Dinah almost sat up to ask her how she had enjoyed the party and if Mark had brought her home, but she didn't want to talk so she shut her eyes again and was fast asleep a few moments later.

She woke up late and found Beth's bed empty. Dinah scrambled out of her own bed and put on a dressing-gown. She found her sister eating cornflakes with sliced banana sprinkled over them. Dinah averted her eyes from the nauseating sight; she sat down with a sigh and poured herself some of the hot coffee Beth had on the table. The last thing she wanted was food.

'Well, you look like the morning after the night before,' Beth said, giggling. 'Great party, wasn't it? I heard about your swim, was it fun?'

Dinah eyed her through slitted lids. 'No, it was not fun,' she said with considerable bitterness. 'I had to come home in an odd collection of Mark's old clothes; I might have got arrested for vagrancy if a policeman had seen me.'

Beth seemed to find that very funny. She had finished her cornflakes and was looking around for something else to eat. 'I think I'll have egg and bacon,' she said and Dinah shuddered.

'Think of all that cholosterol!'

'Yum yum,' Beth said, cracking an egg into a cup.

'Did Mark tell everyone?' Dinah asked, watching her sister lay some rashers of bacon on the grill.

Beth grinned round at her. 'He told me, I don't think he made it one of the party jokes. Oh, don't worry so much—nobody will even remember what happened by Monday, you know what parties are like, once they're over they're forgotten. And anyway, what's so terrible about falling in a goldfish pond fully dressed?' She started to laugh again at Dinah's expression. 'I do wish I'd been there, though. That would be a snapshot for the family album. It was quite a night. What else did you get up to?'

Dinah decided to leave that unanswered. 'Never mind me—what did you do after I'd gone?'

Beth was very busy frying her egg, she didn't seem to hear, so Dinah repeated her question and her sister shrugged without looking at her.

'Oh, the usual party games—dancing, getting chatted up and so on.'

It was the so on that interested Dinah but she could tell Beth was not in a communicative mood. Who had been chatting her up? Mark? Or had it been Max Tracy?

'Mark bring you home?' she asked casually and Beth nodded. Dinah relaxed a little; she didn't want to sound too curious or Beth would probably clam up altogether and so long as her sister hadn't spent much time with Max last night nothing else mattered. She dared not mention Max; Beth might pick up something. She decided to let the matter drop, so she went off to have a bath while Beth was eating her egg and bacon, and then got dressed in order to do some shopping. When she went off with her shopping basket and a list of things they needed Beth was still sitting about in a dressing-gown listening to Radio One. When Dinah got back laden with food and household items, though, the flat was empty, Beth had gone, leaving a note on the kitchen table. Back late tonight, it said, and Dinah read it several times with a worried face. Now what did that mean? Where had Beth gone and with whom? And why hadn't she mentioned that she was going out all day? She usually did; it was part of their plan for living that they should give warning of their weekend plans.

Dinah did not like it.

CHAPTER FOUR

THE sun was flooding in at the office windows, making it hard for Dinah to concentrate on the script she was drafting; it was only a rough working script to take with her when she went to interview Adam Stuart and she would normally have had no problems deciding which line to follow, but for some reason she wasn't thinking too clearly today, no doubt because of that sunshine. She drew down the blinds a little more, deepening the bars of shade on the opposite wall, then sank back into her chair with a sigh which was more like a groan.

The truth was she had too much on her mind; and none of it related to her work. Her cool relations with Quinn had become an open feud; they rarely spoke and when they did Quinn used a barbed mockery she found maddening, especially as he had the knack of making everyone around her laugh so that Dinah's lack of amusement made her the odd one out and gave the impression that she had no sense of humour. Dinah could have weathered that, though; she preferred Quinn Howard at a distance, it didn't disarm him but it went some way to neutralising the shock of his presence. What was really bothering Dinah was Beth. What was her sister up to? During the two weeks since the party Dinah had scarcely seen Beth; she was gone early in the morning and came home very late most days. Normally Beth talked about her crowded love life with cheerful frankness; she never asked Dinah's advice but she was not the secretive type. If Beth was in love the whole world had to know it.

'Busy time at college?' Dinah dared to ask once and got her head snapped off.

'Don't do a time and motion study on me! You do your work, I'll do mine.' Beth had flounced out and Dinah had sighed.

She knew all the signs by now: the euphoria when Beth whistled and sang around the flat with a face like the sun; the black depression when the beloved didn't ring, the rush to the door when the post came, the stampede to the phone when it rang, and then the slumped shoulders and irritability when it was never him.

Their flat was littered with the fall out of her previous love affairs; books on philosophy she never read after she had stopped dating a philosophy student, jazz records she never played after the amateur trumpet player chucked her, the stamp collection into which no stamp had been stuck since she quarrelled with the bearded youth with pimples who had been a keen philatalist. Beth's love life could be tracked without trouble through the discarded hobbies she had once been mad about.

So Dinah was sure now that Beth was in love; the emotional signposts were too obvious, but she hugged her love affair like a baby with a security blanket, she wasn't talking. There were new books around, though; she was reading the latest memoirs of a famous actor and spent a whole Sunday afternoon cooking a very hot curry although she had always hated curry.

'When did you start liking curry?' Dinah had asked mildly, tasting it at her invitation. 'I thought you hated it?'

'I can change my mind, can't I?' Beth had merely muttered.

Who do I know who loves curry and reads memoirs; theatre memoirs, at that? Dinah had wondered. She picked up other clues. Beth usually wore a dress or a skirt and shirt, when she went out these days. She only wore her jeans around the flat. She had bought a couple of stylish dresses from a good-as-new shop and wasn't above borrowing Dinah's clothes, either. She did her hair differently, it was smoother and more sophisticated. Beth was trying to look more mature. Was the guy an older man?

That worried Dinah. Beth was volatile and emotional and her secrecy about this man made Dinah suspect he might be married. Some women might be able to handle a love affair with a married man, but Beth didn't have that sort of toughness. She would get hurt; she would torture herself with doubts and regrets. Perhaps she was already going through a bad time, which would explain her fits of depression. That sort of relationship always ended messily; someone always got hurt and Dinah didn't want it to be her sister. She wished Beth would confide in her, but she couldn't press her.

She had secrets of her own, she didn't want to talk to Beth about Max Tracy, she never had told

Beth about him. She hadn't talked to anyone about what he had done to her; she had been too humiliated. So how could she force Beth's confidence when, in her shoes, she would be as reluctant to talk?

'I'm going down to the canteen for lunch,' a voice said and Dinah started, looking round. Angela stood in the doorway, her face amused as she saw Dinah's abstracted expression. 'Sorry, did I interrupt a train of thought?'

'There isn't one,' Dinah said wryly. 'I might as well break for lunch myself, I'm getting nowhere with this stuff.' She picked up her handbag and rose. 'I must go to the cloakroom first but I think I'll eat in the canteen, too, and then dash out to do some shopping.'

In the cloakroom mirror her eyes slid sideways to view Angela's reflection; the other girl was tidying her blonde curls and didn't notice Dinah's inspection, or see the faint envy in her eyes. Dinah would have liked to have hair of that sunny shade, Angela had a curvy sexiness which made an instant impact with the opposite sex. She wouldn't need to suspect their motives; the way their eyes grew glazed when they stared at her made their motives obvious. Angela was lucky.

She suddenly noticed Dinah's gaze and smiled cheerfully. 'Oh, Patrick Forbes will do the Adam Stuart camera work, but he wasn't keen on the idea, said he hates the guy.'

'You don't surprise me. Patrick has strong views about everything and he detests professional actors, hates filming them. He has a passion for cinema verité—he likes to film in the streets with people who don't know how to act for a camera, what he calls "real people". He won't arrange what he's filming; he likes it to have its own shape and reality. Some producers won't work with him; he's too opinionated, a guy with an obsession, but I rather like his individual approach and no one can dispute that he's a brilliant cameraman. The trouble is, he really wants to dictate what goes into a film, he isn't co-operative.'

'You can say that again. I had quite a time persuading him to do this job. He said he'd only do it for you.' Angela smiled at her.

Dinah laughed. 'Did he? That's flattering.'

They queued up at the counter to get their food. Dinah looked without enthusiasm at the choice of dishes then chose a salad with thin curls of sliced ham.

'Will you be free to come with me to interview Adam Stuart?' she asked Angela who, as she had expected, looked dubious.

'Well, I'd love to, of course, I think he's terrific but I don't know how I'll be placed.'

'I'd like to have you with me,' Dinah said mildly without putting on too much pressure.

They carried their trays over to an empty table and ate their lunch next to a trio of heavily made-up Vikings with horned helmets who drank lemon tea and talked with one eye on the clock, obviously having rushed down during a break in filming some epic up in the main studio. The canteen was usually crowded with odd-looking people, Dinah only spared them a brief glance because she knew one of them slightly. He grinned, waving a hand, and she smiled back. Angela didn't even do that, she was talking about a pair of shoes she had seen and couldn't afford to buy.

Angela stopped talking abruptly, her mouth wide open as she stared across the canteen. Dinah followed the direction of her eyes, wondering what had made Angela look as though she was in a state of trance. Her body went rigid as she realised who Angela was staring at, she hurriedly looked back at her half-eaten meal, her hands shaky as she used her knife and fork. What was Max Tracy doing in the canteen? Was he working here at the moment? She frowned as she remembered Mark saying they had brought Max in for a new drama; she lowered her eyes—she didn't want to catch his eye.

'I must get back to my script,' she said, pushing away her plate.

'Aren't you going to have coffee?' Angela seemed puzzled. She couldn't have heard any gossip about Dinah and Max Tracy; thank heavens for that. Ever since she saw him at Mark's party Dinah had been nervously expecting someone to say something to her about him; if Quinn Howard knew that she had once had an affair with Max then presumably a lot of other people at Metro knew about it. Dinah writhed in torment at the idea of being gossiped about, especially over Max's treatment of her. It was bad enough to have been used and then discarded like an outworn shoe, but it would be a hundred times worse to be aware that people were whispering about her all over the building.

'Yes, I'll get some from the machine upstairs,' Dinah said, walking away. 'See you.'

'I thought you were going shopping,' Angela said curiously but Dinah didn't stop to answer that. She wanted to get away before Max noticed her. She had thought that her affair with him was forgotten about; she had buried it in the past and she didn't want it resurrected publicly but if people saw her and Max together, even exchanging a casual word in the canteen in passing, they would be agog with avid curiosity and immediately believe that the old affair was on again.

John Mower was in the lift; he gave her an acid little smile. 'Busy?' He made it sound like sarcasm but Dinah decided to take the question seriously.

'Hectic,' she agreed with a happy smile which was only skin deep. 'But so long as we get good programmes out of it, I can bear it.'

John's lips curled back from his teeth; it wasn't much of a smile but he was controlling his urge to bite her so she smiled back with cloying good humour, enjoying the frustration in his eyes.

'You mustn't overdo it,' he said. 'I'd hate to see you burn out. You wouldn't be the first bright young thing to do that through pushing themselves too hard.'

'How sweet of you,' Dinah said as she walked out of the lift. He was repeating Quinn Howard's arguments; that was their new line and they would harp on it until they thought of a new attack, but it wasn't going to do them any good.

Dinah walked into her office and sat down behind her desk, her fingers drumming on the script she had abandoned before going to lunch. She scowled out of the window. Why *were* they all so dead against the idea of a woman succeeding in her career? Did it undermine their own egos? What threat did she pose to them all? Was it unconscious, an instinctive almost atavistic reaction, some throwback to an era when sexual roles were fixed and immutable? Did they know why they felt like that? Or did they convince themselves with specious reasoning that they were trying to nudge her out of her job for her own good?

They veered between angry attack on her and a paternal manner which came close to being condescending; if they felt she was winning they bristled, if they thought they had scored some point they patted her on the head as if she was a little girl. The one redeeming factor was that Dinah didn't feel it was personal; anyone in her position would get the same treatment. She could afford to ignore them while she was safe in her present position; but if she ever tried to move higher in the company she was grimly aware that the pressure would become far more intense. Any woman who tried to operate in a large company dominated by men had to be twice as good and work twice as hard as any of her male competitors. In spite of laws about sexual equality it was tougher at the top for women; there were fewer jobs, for a start, and more men pushing for them. A woman started with a built-in disadvantage: her sex.

Dinah was ambitous but sometimes when she looked ahead and realised how hard her road would be if she tried to rise in the company, she felt her spirits sink. It would be so much easier for a man with similar ability and talent to her own. He would just have to prove *himself*, not vault the obstacle of his sex. For a man that further obstacle did not exist. Even if she moved to another company her life wouldn't be any easier; there were plenty of women working on the lower levels in TV but the higher you looked the fewer women you could see and on the topmost levels of all there were almost none. If a woman was appointed to a top post it made headlines.

It was little different in other careers, of course; but Dinah was only interested in her own. She could not see what difference her sex made— a good programme was a good programme, whether it was made by a man or a woman.

She looked down at the script, grimacing. She really must concentrate, she didn't want to go along to meet Adam Stuart without having done her homework on him. It would waste valuable time, she would then have to take up half the interview exploring his background without knowing which areas she should pinpoint. That approach always made for a messy jigsaw puzzle when you came to edit the film you had shot. It was cheaper and quicker to know what you wanted before you arrived with your cameras.

She had done some research in the clippings library and managed to see all the TV interviews which Adam had done, there were only a few and all of those came from the States. As far as the UK was concerned he was almost an unknown story; in spite of his fame and the success of his films. The media had had far too little to go on, they had only run current stories on him, mostly on his love.life and the money he was making. Dinah wanted to do something different, as well as slotting his life into the general theme of her series. Breaking new ground was always more exciting than following a well-worn trail.

There was a tap on her door half-an-hour later. She had become completely absorbed in her script and lifted her head in blank amazement as Max came into the office.

'I've tracked you down to your lair,' he said, smiling as easily as though she must be delighted to see him. Dinah stared, sitting very upright, her hands clenching on her script. He was wearing a white suit with a waistcoat which hugged his slim waist; he looked as though he had just stepped off the set of a musical. He was too good-looking to be real; that blond hair smooth and perfectly styled, his skin tanned, so evenly that she suspected the tan came from a bottle or from lying on a sunbed for hours, his features too perfect. He strolled towards her, one eyebrow quizzically lifted. That was a new trick, she thought, it probably went down well in a film but in real life it was very overdone, and so was the charm which was so cloying that it might have come from a bottle, too.

'Surprised to see me?' he asked and she leaned back in her chair, tapping a finger on her script.

'Amazed. Don't you understand English? I

thought I'd made it clear I didn't want to see you again. Nobody plays the same trick on me twice.'

He perched on the edge of her desk, looking at her with what she recognised as a carefully contrite expression. Max had learnt how to use that over-perfect set of features to miraculous effect—the lift of an eyebrow, the trace of a smile, and he could convey oceans of meaning. He would probably have made it in television without her help but he hadn't had the patience to wait.

'That's why I have to talk to you,' he said seriously, leaning towards her. 'You've got it all wrong, I was stunned when I realised what you thought. When we first met I didn't even know you worked in television and it never entered my head that you might have any influence. After all, you weren't important, Dinah, you didn't have any pull. How could you think I used you as a ladder? That's what you said, wasn't it? The idea's crazy. I dated you because I liked you, I had no ulterior motives.'

'Then why did you drop me as soon as you had got a foot in TV?' she asked drily.

'I told you why. You and I had no future then; I had no money and a long way to go before I could say I was succeeding, and you were just starting your own career too. It seemed wisest to fade out of your life. Don't you remember telling me that Mark had warned you about burning the candle at both ends? I thought you were giving me a hint, I thought *you* wanted to end it.' He made a wry face. 'And to tell the absolute truth, you were too much of a distraction—I liked you too much and I felt I needed more elbow room. It wasn't the right time for me to get that involved with anyone. I'd already realised that it was getting too serious but I didn't want to lose you, it was only when you told me that you'd had a warning from Mark that I decided to do my vanishing act.'

Dinah considered him soberly, wondering how much truth there was in what he had said and completely uncertain. Most people prefer to view their own actions and motives in a flattering light; they deceive themselves as much as they do other people and are hurt when anyone challenges them. Max was a vain man; he wouldn't enjoy knowing that she despised him. He smiled at her pleadingly. That smile had once made her heart stop but now her heart obstinately went on beating without a pause.

'I didn't mean to hurt you,' he said, and she flushed.

'I wasn't hurt! Disillusioned, maybe.' The lie seemed justified; after all she couldn't let Max think he had knocked the bottom out of her world when he walked away from her. Her pride wouldn't take that.

'Have dinner with me,' he asked, smiling as he ran a hand over his smooth blond hair. He was far too conscious of his looks, he knew people did a double-take in amazement when they saw him. All his life Max must have watched women giving at the knees when he turned his smile in their direction. 'We have a lot of water under the bridge to talk about.'

'I'm sorry, I have a date tonight,' she said, lying again.

'When, then? I'm working at Metro all this week, any evening will do.'

She gestured to the script under her hands. 'I'm afraid I can't spare any time this week, I'm up to my ears in work.'

He looked down and his eyes skimmed over a few words. 'Is that the programme on Adam Stuart your sister told me about? She's gorgeous, isn't she? I never met her when I was seeing you but I remember you mentioning her. She's got tremendous personality.'

Dinah picked up something odd about his tone; it was too casual and his profile seemed slightly tense, as though he was controlling something, hiding something. Was she imagining it?

He slid down off the desk and walked around the room looking at her filing cabinets, the posters on the walls, the plants lined up on the window sill.

'I had the devil of a job to find your office—there's no name on your door.'

'That's so that if they kick me out, they won't have to spend money having a new name plate made,' she said absently, wondering what he had really thought of Beth. He couldn't be the guy Beth was dating, could he? Beth wouldn't be such a fool. Or would she? After all, Max was plausible, very attractive, a man women fell for easily. Dinah had made a fool of herself over him, why shouldn't Beth? Dinah stared at him anxiously, wishing she could see past that beautiful mask. Why was he here? What was he up to?

He had looked round at her, his face almost shocked. 'You've got very cynical.'

'Maybe I have good reasons,' she said, still wishing she could work out his motives for wanting to see her. If he was pursuing her sister would he want to date her too? Even Max wouldn't be that two-faced; he was too clever. He would know that sooner or later his game would explode in his face; one of them would find out about the other and then the fat would be in the fire. Or was he planning some complicated manoeuvre? If he was chasing Beth was he afraid that Dinah would warn her sister about him? Was he hoping to placate Dinah to clear his way in order to chase Beth?

It was all too complicated, Dinah shrugged the possibilities aside. The only certain facts were that Max was here, he was trying to make friends with her again and that just now he had been over casual when he mentioned Beth. You could weave those facts into any number of patterns, who knew which was the right one?

'Was it me who made you cynical?' he asked as though he cared and she gave him a dry smile.

'No, it was working here.' He had been part of it; but she knew that there was a lot more to it than that.

He looked at his watch, making a face. 'I'm due back on the studio floor in five minutes. I must go. We're rehearsing for a take. The director keeps saying we'll go for a first take with every scene but it never works out like that. He's a nitpicker.' He walked to the door, stood there hesitating. 'Have dinner with me one night this week, Dinah. Please.'

She hesitated, and at that instant Quinn Howard loomed up in the corridor behind Max, staring past his shoulder at Dinah with a contemptuous expression which acted on her like a spur on an uncertain horse. She stiffened, jerking upright, meeting his eyes angrily, then gave Max a false smile.

'Okay, tomorrow night?'

He looked triumphant. 'Wonderful, I'll pick you up here, shall I? Say at six-thirty? We'll have a drink before we eat.' Max's eyes had that familiar brightness. He thought he had talked her round, was going to get his own way with her and it didn't really surprise him because Max thought that he was irresistible, women would always melt in the fire of his sex appeal, even when he had treated them as badly as he had treated Dinah. Her capitulation convinced him that he had sold her his story about why he had dropped her last time, but Dinah wasn't buying it. She wasn't sure how much of it to believe but she didn't really care, either way. She had been wildly in love with him three years ago, but she had grown up a lot since then. Now she didn't even like him, the only emotion she felt for Max was disbelief that he had ever got to her, he was a phoney and a fake, his surface glitter wasn't even skin deep.

'Six-thirty, that's fine,' she said, very aware of Quinn's hard stare. She didn't like the way he was watching her, that was one reason why she had accepted Max's invitation. Quinn Howard had no right to look at her with angry scorn. What affair of his was it whether she went out with Max or not?

Her other reason was less impulsive; she wanted to find out whether it was Max who was dating Beth.

She didn't know quite what she would do if she found her suspicions were correct, but from bitter experience she knew that Max Tracy could be a disaster for any woman who got involved with him: if Beth was seeing him secretly, there could be a rough time ahead for her.

'I'll look forward to it,' Max said and blew her a kiss. He almost walked straight into Quinn as he turned away. 'Oh, hallo!' he said and Quinn gave him a curt nod. He didn't say anything and after a brief hesitation Max vanished.

Quinn came into the office and closed the door. He leaned on it and stared at her. Dinah lifted her chin in defiance, leaving it to him to speak first. She had nothing to say to him, nothing she meant to say, that was—her mind was buzzing with a few angry thoughts she would have loved to voice, but suppressed because if she lost her temper with him she might say a little too much.

'I didn't have you down as a weak-kneed fool,' he said with a force which made her nerves jerk. 'What are you? A masochist? That smooth-talking pretty boy took you for a ride and dumped you, didn't he? Are you really going to give him the chance to do it again?'

'Don't you float into my office like a little black rain cloud,' Dinah said, pretending to yawn. 'Go and rain on someone else.'

He came away from the door in three strides; she got the feeling he only stopped because her desk was in his way otherwise he might have walked right on out of the window and she would have cheered as he fell out.

'Women baffle me,' he said in a harsh outburst.

'You surprise me. I thought we were an open book to you.'

'What has he got? What do you find so irresistible?'

She looked down at her desk, shrugging. 'I'm busy, go and play twenty questions with Angela. She may like it. I don't. My private life is none of your business.'

He inhaled, breathing fiercely, anger coming off him like radiation and the geiger counter of her female instincts picked it up and clicked with frenetic awareness. When he threw something at her she jumped, flinching, as though she had been expecting some violence, but the plastic bag that landed on her desk looked harmless enough and she stared at it blankly.

'What's this?'

'Your shoes,' he said. 'I retrieved them from Mark's goldfish pond and have had them cleaned.' He sounded so angry the words were an accusation more than an explanation.

Dinah was too surprised to say anything at first, she pulled her shoes out of the bag, staggered to see that they looked as good as new. Their immersion hadn't ruined them; she had wiped them out of her memory because she thought a few hours in a weedy pond would render them unwearable but they showed no sign of what had happened to them, the fragile white leather smooth and well-polished.

Flushed, she looked up then. 'Thank you, that

was very thoughtful of you, I don't know what to say.'

'Thank you will do,' he said tightly then gave a ragged frown, his black brows meeting. 'No, it won't,' he said, his tone suddenly changing. He moved round her desk and bent and kissed her hard, driving her head back, and Dinah's hands clutched at the edge of her desk as she felt an overwhelming surge of excitement. She struggled not to respond but her lips were trembling and her eyes wouldn't stay open. Quinn's hand slid down over her breast, warm against the thin silk blouse she wore, and she angrily felt the stir and tumult of desire begin in her flesh. Perhaps Quinn was right, perhaps she was some sort of masochist or why would she feel this clamour in the blood for a man cut out of the same cloth as Max Tracy? Quinn had just used an icily cutting tone when he talked about Max but he was just as unscrupulous, just as intent on using her sexuality as a weapon against her merely to further his own career.

Tears pricked below her closed lids, she pushed him away with a violence that forced him to release her and he straightened. Dinah shot to her own feet and stood with her back to him, looking out of the window. She didn't want him to see her wet eyes or to realise how upset she was—she wouldn't give him that satisfaction.

'Get out of here,' she whispered shakily, her arms folded in a gesture of self-defence across her breasts. Bitterness burned in her throat. Was she fated to be attracted by men whose only interest in her was to deceive, humiliate, use her? What was wrong with her? She had never encouraged Quinn to think she would be a pushover, she didn't flirt with him or give him the beckoning, alluring little smiles that Angela showered at random among the men in the company. Angela's smiles didn't mean much but she frankly confessed that she enjoyed flirting, she did it automatically every time an attractive man appeared on the horizon, and the men obviously enjoyed Angela's company. If Angela got kissed it was because she invited it. Dinah had never invited Quinn to come a step too close; she had hoisted a no-boarders signal right from the start. Quinn's mocking smiles and lazy observation of her had only infuriated her. When had she started to be vulnerable to him? Why was she trembling and struggling with tears over someone she angrily despised?

She heard the door close and knew she was alone. Quinn hadn't said a word, just gone in silence. It was some relief to know he hadn't realised what that kiss had done to her; Dinah wasn't even certain herself why she felt so keyed up and tense just because Quinn Howard had kissed her. She ran a hand over her wet eyes, sniffing like a child. She didn't want to know, either, she insisted to the inner voice which kept asking questions she did not want to face.

CHAPTER FIVE

DINAH sat in the kitchen next morning drinking black coffee and staring blankly at the sunlight patterning the wall while she tried to wake herself up. She had slept badly, partly because she had had one ear cocked to pick up the sound of Beth coming home. She hadn't had a chance to talk to Beth last night, her sister had been out all evening and Dinah had fallen asleep around one o'clock without having heard Beth's key turning in the lock. This morning Dinah's eyes were heavy, her mind troubled. While she waited for Beth to come home she had spent a great deal too much time thinking about Quinn and her own inexplicable depression after he kissed her.

She couldn't understand it, her own feelings baffled her. She didn't like the man, any more than she trusted him. Was her brain going? It was such a simple equation, one she had made instinctively and unconsciously the minute he appeared at Metro—Quinn reminded her of Max Tracy and she had learnt indelibly that men like Max were all phoney glamour on the outside and cold-blooded ambition on the inside. When she first saw Max at Mark's party she had felt a stab of pain, but it had been remembered pain, inextricably entwined with a number of other memories—her own humiliation and disillusionment, how other people must have seen it, her wounded pride at knowing what everyone must be thinking, her angry resentment and determination never to be so vulnerable again. Max had talked very plausibly in her office yesterday but deep inside herself she did not believe him and she would never trust him again. Only a fool makes the same mistake twice and that applied as much to the way she thought about Quinn as to how she regarded Max. She wouldn't let herself believe in Quinn, either.

Her tears in the office yesterday made her burn with self-contempt. How could she have been so stupid? A man she despises kisses her and she starts crying! How ridiculous could you get? Quinn had told her she was weak-kneed for accepting a date with Max; he might as well have been talking about himself. She was only going to dinner with Max because she wanted to know if it was him seeing Beth in secret, but her tears when Quinn kissed her had had no sane motive, they had risen behind her eyelids without explanation, without her expecting or understanding them, it was shameful, she hated herself.

Her hands tightened around her cup of coffee as she heard the bathroom door bang. Beth was up! Dinah had left her sleeping, curled round on her side with a hand under her pink, relaxed face on the pillow. Beth had been smiling in her sleep, a faint dimple denting the side of her mouth. She had looked like a child and Dinah's heart had ached as she watched her. If Beth was involved with Max Tracy she was going to get hurt, Dinah couldn't bear the thought. It made her angry and anxious and determined to find a way of making sure it did not happen, although she couldn't yet work out how she would do that.

Beth flew into the kitchen a few moments later wearing jeans and a V-necked top. 'I'm going to be late,' she said looking at the clock. She dumped a bulging case of books on the table, grabbed a cereal bowl and poured cornflakes into it before adding milk and sugar, poured herself coffee and sat down with the air of one who is going to eat fast and run, perched right on the edge of her chair and beginning to push spoonfuls of cornflakes into her mouth immediately. 'Got a lecture,' she said, the words muffled.

'Going out again tonight?' Dinah asked casually. That was what she wanted to know, that was why she had waited for Beth to get up this morning and had hoped to talk to her last night. If Beth was dating Max she wouldn't be seeing him tonight because he would be taking Dinah to dinner.

Beth shook her head, grimacing. 'I've got to do an essay, I'm behind with my work so I'm having a quiet night tonight.'

Dinah's heart sank so much she was scarcely able to hide it. She looked down into her black coffee, fighting to keep her face serene.

'And no lectures!' Beth said aggressively, misreading her expression. 'I work hard all day, I'm entitled to some fun now and then. All work and no play, you know the old saying. I try to space it out; I've every intention of getting my degree.'

Dinah got up, she still could not speak and she

did not want her sister to start wondering why she was so pale, she had felt the colour leaving her face when Beth admitted she was not going out tonight.

'Don't sulk,' Beth flung after her. 'I hate people who think things they don't say and go around with faces as long as fiddles.'

'I'm not sulking,' Dinah said huskily. 'I'm just in a hurry. See you, I must dash.'

She had to stand all the way to her stop on the underground; the train was packed with people squashed up together, strap-hanging in a perspiring silence because the June heatwave had not died away and there was no air in the crowded train. When she emerged she was sticky with heat and already felt tired. The traffic fumes seemed more poisonous than ever, they hung around in the hot air, there was no wind to move them upward. Everyone was wearing the minimum of clothing possible for city wear, people were beginning to complain about the weather now that their first surprised enjoyment of it had become a longing to feel a little cooler. It was hard to work when you were so hot, your mind couldn't concentrate, it was more occupied with physical discomfort than anything else, even walking around the Metro offices had become an endurance test because with every step you felt sweat break out on your skin. There was no air-conditioning in the building; all the windows were wide open but little air circulated because the air outside in the streets was so still and heavy, languorous and oppressive, weighted with the scents of petrol fumes and dust, the smell of hot fat and cooking food from the cheap restaurants around the district.

Dinah sat at her desk with the window blinds drawn down and the top buttons of her shirt undone, trying to arrange interviews for her second programme by phone, in between dictating letters to Angela and talking to Patrick Forbes, the freelance camera man who was coming with her to film Adam Stuart. Patrick was a husky young man with impatient black eyes and rough brown hair which looked as though he never brushed it or ran a comb through it. He intensified this impression by constantly tugging at his untidy locks with one hand when he talked as though he needed to relieve his irritation some how.

Dinah liked him because he always treated her with casual equality, never patronising her or becoming aggressive, her sex never entered into their relationship, she got no cheap sexist chat, no innuendo or snide jibes from Patrick. He was obsessed with what he saw through his view-finder, he looked to frame life, freeze it, arrange and pattern it as though everything around him was living material in an untidy jumble he was driven to sort out and present more rationally.

'You want to be God,' Dinah accused and he brushed that aside with a wild gesture. Patrick was rarely still for long, he was possessed with energy he had to release into the air. His hair crackled with life, his eyes glowed with it. He had no sense of humour about himself or his work; when he did laugh it was usually at a banana skin joke of the physical kind. He roared with laughter when someone skidded and fell over in a puddle, he chuckled when Dinah wryly told him how she had fallen into Mark's pond, he grinned at her description of herself shuffling home in Mark's baggy jeans and shoes. Humour, for Patrick, had to be very broad and obvious.

'I'm only doing this job with Stuart to oblige you,' he told her bluntly. 'I wouldn't do it for anyone else; the man's a bore. I hate actors, you can't get near them, they're too busy trying to look beautiful, they hide themselves. I've no time for masks. My job is to rip them off but actors are too good at hanging on to their masks.' His black eyes snapped. 'I saw that new guy—Tracy—as I came in here this morning. He's another of the same type. Posing bastard. All they are is on the top, there's nothing underneath.'

'All the same, Stuart has a very interesting background—what I'm after is where he came from, how he got to where he is.'

'Rags to riches,' Patrick said, writhing with disgust. 'Tell me the old, old story.'

'That wasn't what I meant exactly,' she protested. 'I'm not interested so much in the glamorous life he leads now. I want to get him talking about his childhood.'

Patrick eyed her derisively. 'Then why are we filming in this country house he has rented? Why not in wherever he came from? The slums, was it? Now I'd go for that, taking him back ... I don't know though, it's still a bit corny.'

'If I can get him talking about it, though, we can slice in film of the places he knew as a child while he's doing a voice-over, and then cut back now and then to the country house and today. Of course it's corny, the best stuff often is—there's nothing new under the sun, is there? If you do your usual brilliant job of interpeting place with the camera, we may have a very good film, though.'

'I'd need a free hand,' Patrick said in a thoughtful, bargaining voice.

'You've got it—so long as the end result matches what Stuart talks about. I have a hunch that he's sensitive about his childhood, he seems touchy, I may have trouble getting him to talk freely about it and if his resentment comes over the way I hope it will we could get some powerful stuff.'

Patrick stared at nothing, his brow corrugated. 'I wonder . . . how would it be if we switched to black and white for the flashback part of the film? That would make it more effective, it's exciting to work in black and white, sharpens the definitions like nobody's business. I could do a great job with slum streets and filthy old tenements filmed without colour—it would really point up the other side of the picture.'

Dinah stared at his intent face, a quiver of excitement darting through her. She felt so tired today, it was difficult to put real enthusiasm into her discussion with Patrick, but even through her weariness his idea seemed fascinating.

'What do you think?' he asked, his black eyes flashing back to her face.

'It's certainly a great idea—can we leave a decision on it until we see what we get from the interview?'

Patrick did not like her discreet hesitation, he wanted her to agree there and then, his face grew sulky.

'You said I could have a free hand, I might have known you were just spouting hot air. I like the idea, it would be worth doing this tedious job just to get the chance of experimenting with a colour switch.'

'I didn't say we wouldn't do it, I just asked you to wait until we've done the interview,' she said hurriedly. You expected temperament in actors but cameramen like Patrick had it too; half Dinah's job was keeping everyone she worked with happy. Tact was essential if you weren't to have continual problems with people who felt they were not being treated properly.

'In the meantime I'll do some research on the way that part of London looked when Stuart was a boy,' Patrick decided. 'I'll look up newspaper files and old documentary clippings—it wouldn't be a bad idea to slot a few stills into the flashbacks.'

Dinah gave him a wry look. She could see that Patrick was already edging himself into her job, trying to take over the producer's role. She was going to have to watch him but she left any clash until a later stage. He was more than capable of pulling out and then she would have to find a new camera team. Patrick worked with some very skilful technicians, she wasn't likely to get anyone better. It was wiser to do the interview before she started arguing with Patrick about how the film should be structured.

She had lunch with Mark and several writers at

the famous restaurant Simpsons in the Strand, where the roast beef speciality was a favourite dish of Mark's. He watched greedily as pink slices fell from the knife of the waiter serving the beef which was wheeled to the table in a vast silver dish with a domed cover. The atmosphere was businesslike, most of the customers men and the food very English, mainly roast meats and heavy English puddings, suet or sponge with jam or treacle poured over them, or rice pudding with sultanas. It reminded Dinah of the Victorian era, it had the atmosphere of a scene from Dickens, it was a surprise to leave the place and find oneself in the hustle and roar of modern London. Mark hailed a taxi, they said goodbye to the writers and drove back to the Metro building talking in a desultory way about the discussion they had been having. Mark yawned and caught her eye, grinning sheepishly.

'I shouldn't eat heavy lunches, I always want to go to sleep afterwards.' She hadn't seen much of him since his party and her swim in his pond, which he had mentioned over lunch, using it as an amusing anecdote to relax the guests. Dinah had gritted her teeth and pretended to smile but she would be very glad when everyone forgot about the incident.

Mark grinned at her. 'Got your shoes back yet? Quinn fished for them with a shrimping net, did he tell you? Said he would have them cleaned before he gave them back to you.'

'Yes, he gave them to me yesterday,' Dinah said. 'It was nice of him.'

'Don't overdo the gratitude,' Mark teased.

'If it wasn't for him I wouldn't have fallen in!'

Mark looked fascinated. 'What did he do? Push you?'

Dinah looked away. 'Something like that.'

'Why are you blushing?' Mark asked, very amused. 'Don't tell me Quinn made a pass? Did you fight him off and end up in the pond?'

'Oh, don't be absurd,' she snapped.

Mark was delighted. 'I've always suspected he fancied you, he watches you like a hawk.'

'His reasons are not romantic,' Dinah said scathingly. 'He wants my job, he wants my programme—every time I see him he tries to persuade me that the work is too much for me, I'm too delicate for so much strain. You know that as well as I do. Don't tell me that my opposition isn't always nagging you to get rid of me because I wouldn't believe you if you swore it on a stack of Bibles.'

Mark shrugged. 'Someone is always trying to persuade me to do something; this place is a hotbed of intrigue. What makes you think you're special? They tell me poor old Eric is past it, I ought to find a younger guy for his programme. They tell me John has been running the news department for too long, it's time he moved on. People are always pushing, always restless. That's the way they should be. It means they're alive and busy. You take it all too personally. They started trying to get me to drop you the minute I let you make that first programme, and before you leap down my throat with cries of "Anti-feminism!" let me tell you that they'd have been against you whatever your sex. Haven't you realised yet that everyone has an axe to grind? Cut-throat competition is endemic in this business. If you're successful you're bound to attract enemies.'

'But being a woman makes it twice as likely,' Dinah said. 'And makes your enemies twice as poisonous.'

Mark gave her a wry look, and shrugged again. There was a pause then he said: 'I didn't invite Max Tracy to my party, someone brought him along, I had no idea he was going to turn up.'

He didn't look at her as he spoke but Dinah stiffened in angry embarrassment. Mark was tacitly apologising for Max's presence at the party, she would have preferred him to drop the subject and so did not answer, but he went on quietly: 'He was just one of those things that happen to all of us; we all go through a bad scene sometime in our lives.' He paused again and she stared obstinately out of the cab window, staying silent. Mark sighed. 'Your sister didn't know about him, did she?'

That brought Dinah's head round. She looked sharply at him. 'I didn't tell her about Max, no.' She swallowed. 'Did you?' Why had Mark coupled Beth's name with Max? Had he seen something, heard something about them? Dinah knew how quickly gossip flew around the Metro building, people often knew a piece of news which the two people concerned believed to be a deadly secret.

Mark shook his head, looking away, his profile serious. 'I didn't tell her but don't you think she ought to know?'

Dinah struggled not to look as desperately anxious as she felt. 'Why? What has it got to do with Beth? She's not studying ancient history, my extinct love affairs wouldn't interest her.' She waited for his answer in agitation, watching him intently.

It was impossible to read his guarded face, but she was sure he hesitated. 'If you confided in her, she might find it easier to talk to you about whatever is on her mind,' he suggested in a careful voice.

'What makes you think she doesn't?'

Mark shot her a brief glance, his eyes wary. She got the definite feeling that they were fencing, both of them behind shields and probing each other's defences.

'She admires you,' Mark said slowly. 'She seems to think you're very much together, a cool-headed success who knows exactly what she's doing—and that makes it harder for her to talk to you honestly, she's too afraid of having you despise her.'

'Why should I do that?' Dinah asked in a dry little voice, absorbing what he had said about her sister with incredulity—could Beth really see her like that? Had she given Mark that impression or had he simply formed his own conclusions, which could well be wildly off the mark?

The taxi jerked to a stop outside the Metro building and the driver leaned back and opened the door. Dinah climbed out and waited while Mark paid the fare, then they walked across the pavement together.

'Why don't you try talking to her?' Mark said

lightly as he followed her into the building. Their footsteps sounded hollow on the stone flooring. They went into the lift behind a group of other people and did not talk on the way up. Dinah was worried, what was Mark getting at? She hated talking about Max Tracy; just remembering the past was enough to make her healed wounds break open and bleed again. She did not like Max, he meant nothing to her now, but the memory of her pain and humiliation had gone too deep to be erased by time. She still burned with the same hypersensitive embarrassment each time she remembered him, but she found even more intolerable the idea of having to watch a re-run of that whole affair but with Beth playing her role. Max was not doing that to her sister. Had Beth confided in Mark? Had he heard something from Max? Why was he dropping heavy hints without coming out with whatever was on his mind? Mark had been very tactful with her three years ago, he had observed what happened, he must have guessed even more, but he hadn't said a word to her either at the time or later. She had been grateful for his kindness and discretion over that, but she found it maddening to be given veiled hints about Beth which could mean anything—or nothing.

John Mower got in at the third floor and murmured a greeting to them both. 'I hear you're having dinner at Number Ten tonight,' he said to Mark who nodded.

'The PM is having a media dinner—most of the Fleet Street editors and a half a dozen TV and radio people. It means I'll have to talk to some of my worst enemies but I'll survive, I suppose. At least the wine should be good.'

Dinah stared at the wall. She would change places with him, she was not looking forward to having dinner with Max. She would have to keep her temper, she would undoubtedly get indigestion because every mouthful would choke her, and she was going to have to phrase everything she said very carefully because if Max was dating Beth he might be wary of everything *he* said, she would only find out the truth by trickery.

She gave Mark and John a vague smile as the lift stopped at her floor, and wandered across the landing to her own office. Angela was typing busily, the phone was ringing, Dinah sat at her desk and wished she felt more like work.

'It's Adam Stuart's publicity people,' Angela told her through the door and Dinah sighed and picked up the phone, hoping he hadn't decided to cancel the interview, and relieved to discover it was only a minor query he wanted to raise about how long the interview would take.

At six-twenty the offices were quiet and mostly empty. Angela had left dead on five-thirty, as she invariably did. Dinah had worked on at her desk trying to ignore the smouldering heat; she began to think a thunderstorm must break to relieve the dragging tension in the air. She was wearing a matching jade green cotton shirt and skirt, she was not taking much trouble for Max Tracy and had no intention of changing into anything more glamorous, but in spite of her aggressive resentment towards him she was nervous, her palms were sweating.

When he appeared in her doorway she felt the back of her neck prickle with tension. He smiled across the office at her. 'Ready?'

She got up without smiling back. Whatever she might tell herself she couldn't feel at ease with him around, she was diminished in his presence. He knew she had been in love with him and that he had rejected her. Love was a war game and the losers were the vanquished, Dinah couldn't forget that, her intelligence might angrily deny it but her emotions still echoed with the pain of the past.

'I've booked a table at L'Opera,' Max said. 'We'll have a drink in a bar in Covent Garden first, if that's okay with you?'

'Fine,' she said, shrugging. She didn't care where they had a drink or where he had booked a table.

Max glanced at her cluttered desk, raising an eyebrow. 'Busy? I suppose you're planning the next series? When do you start filming?'

'In ten days' time.' Dinah walked out of the office and he followed her across the landing into the lift.

'In the studio?' he queried lightly and she shook her head, guessing that he was talking about her work because it was a safe topic of conversation, miles from the personal issues which lay between them like an abyss so deep it would never give up its dead.

But that would be to imagine that Max had some real idea of how much he had once hurt her, not to mention a sense of regret, and Dinah did not believe he had either. No, it was more likely that he was talking about her work in order to put them on a friendly footing again. Max was not a man who would ever care how much he hurt people, she was certain of that.

'I didn't want to film in the studio, it makes it so static—we're interviewing Adam Stuart, at a country house he has rented. He's over here to make a film later this year. He's producing it, as well as playing the leading role, and I suspect he's only giving me this interview because he wants the publicity for his film. I gather he's put a lot of his own money into it; on this one he has a lot to lose.'

She was talking because it was easier than silence. She was afraid of what a silence might hold, of what it might seem to hold, to him. They had been waiting on the pavement outside the Metro building now for several minutes. Max kept trying to hail each taxi which passed but they were always occupied. This was still the rush hour. In an hour or two it would be easier to get taxis but after a time Max gave her a wry glance and said: 'Shall we walk for a while? We may strike lucky on the way.'

They walked briskly, Max didn't look at her very often, he asked casual questions and she answered with equal carelessness, but she felt disembodied, remote. What was she doing here, with him? Why did he want to have dinner with her? What was his motive this time?

A few moments later they managed to get a taxi and while they were driving to Covent Garden she carefully mentioned Beth, watching him out of the corner of her eye. 'She shares my flat now, she's going to university in London.'

'Yes, I know,' he said. 'She told me all about herself at the party—she's not much like you, is she?'

'Isn't she?' Dinah said with an oddly poignant note which she heard herself and wished she could suppress. She hoped Beth was not like her, she hoped Beth could protect herself better, guard herself against pain, but she was not optimistic. Beth was far more vulnerable; she was intense and open, she gave herself to life without reserve and that meant she could get badly hurt.

'No, nothing at all like you,' Max said vehemently, as they got out of the taxi outside an Edwardian bar with stained-glass windows and a swinging sign above the door, painted with a bold-looking mermaid with one eye closed in a wink.

'What will you have?' Max asked as they sat down at one of the round, polished tables in the bar, then he went over to the counter to get their drinks while Dinah looked at the Edwardian prints hanging on the walls, the polished brass pots of tall palms, the rows of pewter tankards arranged for display behind the bar counter.

'Like it?' Max asked, joining her.

'It's a bit pseud.'

He laughed. 'Fake. But fun. It was originally a dirty old place but full of real Edwardian junk— now it has been tarted up and nothing is real.'

'For the tourists,' Dinah said drily. Covent Garden was a tourist trap now; full of antique shops and souvenir shops with a street market full of swag with which to tempt tourists. On most days you could catch a street mime with white face and clown's outfit performing for free, but hoping to be thrown a few pennies; or see some buskers playing trumpets or jugglers sending coloured balls into the air, some days music students played Mozart or jazz, and there were open-air cafés where you could sit and drink coffee while you watched the colourful parade of life going past.

That was what the bar was like, too. It had once been real and full of busy working life, but now it was a tourist trap, and completely phony.

Max talked about the play he was doing at Metro and Dinah listened, then he looked at his watch and said they ought to go and have dinner. As they left the bar she saw some girls staring at him, whispering. They looked excited, they had recognised him. Max smoothed a hand over his blond hair, carefully not noticing them, but Dinah saw a faint smile curve his mouth. He enjoyed being recognised, being stared at with admiration. She saw him glance sideways as they passed a shop window, he was watching his own reflection with satisfaction. Max was what he saw—a beautiful shadow in a glass. He was no more real than the fake Edwardian bar they had just left.

She laughed helplessly and he looked at her in baffled surprise. 'What's funny? Did I miss something?'

'I was laughing at myself,' Dinah said. What a fool she had been, even more of a fool than she had realised until now.

Max curved an eyebrow, smiled with that cloying charm. He was like ice-cream with syrup poured over the top; he set your teeth on edge unless you were too young to feel it. Too young or too stupid—she had been both and so was Beth and Dinah knew then that she had to be frank with Beth, talk to her honestly and tell her what Max had done, what sort of man he was—it would mean admitting her own folly but she couldn't let her pride stand in the way when her sister's happiness was at stake. The only way Beth might believe her was if she held nothing back, she hated the idea of exposing herself to Beth's pity but it would be the only way. Max was too plausible, his charm too convincing.

They had their dinner at L'Opera, not far from where they had had their drink, but in an atmosphere of cloistered opulence which was far more realistically Edwardian, with velvet sofas and soft-footed waiters floating from table to table. Max spent most of the evening talking about himself and his blossoming career, he wasn't seriously interested in anything else. He told her he had had offers from Hollywood, chances to star in long-running TV serials, fabulous sums waved at him to tempt him to do this or that commercial. Scripts showered on him every day, but he preferred, he said, to bide his time, choose the right ones. He could afford to wait for the perfect opportunity.

'I'm in no hurry,' he said and she knew he was making it very clear that he didn't need anybody's help now. Perhaps that was why he had wanted to see her again, he wanted to show her just that; admit tacitly that he had needed her once, used her to get into the right company, meet the important people he had needed to know, but that he didn't need her any more, he had made it and now the important people came looking for him instead of the other way around. Max had a brand of pride; he might be ready to use people to get to the top but he preferred to boast that he had done it on his own, without anybody's help. He was happier telling her that he was so much in demand that he could pick and choose parts than he would be admitting that he wasn't succeeding, he needed help. He hadn't told her that frankly when he first met her three years ago; if he had said: help me meet people! would she have agreed? Probably. But Max hadn't been honest, he had been devious, oblique, because that was his nature, when he went after something he went sideways, disguising his intention.

She sensed, too, that he was enjoying himself; she had known him when he was desperate to get somewhere, a total unknown, and he was getting a big kick out of showing her how far he had come in three years. Max was an actor and she was the audience he wanted, someone who could really appreciate his success because they had known him before it happened.

Every so often she managed to mention Beth, always watching him, and getting no real idea how he was reacting. He was too good an actor.

It was very late when he took her home in a taxi. Outside her flat he took her hand and looked soulfully into her eyes. 'It's been marvellous,' he said and for him she had the feeling that it had been—Max had had a great time telling her about his success.

'Thank you for the dinner, it was splendid,' she said. The food had been excellent; what a pity she had been too absorbed in other things to enjoy it.

'Now that I've found you again, I refuse to lose you,' Max said in a deep warm voice pitched perfectly. Once that voice had sent shivers down her back, now she smiled at him drily and didn't answer. 'I should never have lost you in the first place, I was a fool. Tonight was wonderful, we must do it again soon. I'm going to a party on Saturday, why don't you come?'

Dinah wasn't listening. She was watching a man walking out of the building in which she had her flat. At her first glance she hadn't recognised him, then she had done a double-take. What was Quinn doing here? He walked a little way down the street and got into a parked car.

'Will you come?' Max asked, unaware that she wasn't even with him any more. She watched Quinn drive away; her heart beating slowly, heavily. 'Your hands are cold,' Max said. 'You must be tired, am I keeping you up late?'

She pulled her hands away, muttered: 'Goodnight, Max,' and shot out of the taxi. Max leaned out, calling: 'What about the party?' and she shook her head and ran into the hallway of the apartment block. She heard the taxi drive off and stood there, looking at her watch. It was gone midnight. Her mind worked as if it was grinding to a halt. Quinn had been here, where else could he have been but in her flat with Beth? It would be too much of a coincidence if he had been visiting someone else.

She fumbled for her key, very slowly walked to the door of her flat. It was difficult to get the key into the lock, her hands were shaking so much. Quinn had been here, alone with Beth, at midnight. She had been wildly wrong in her guesswork, it hadn't been Max, he hadn't caused the magnetic excitement, the euphoric radiance of love in Beth's face or the sudden depressions when the phone didn't ring. Beth's secrecy had had another reason, she knew that Dinah and Quinn were enemies, she knew Dinah wouldn't like it if she found out that her sister was dating him.

Dinah put a hand to her mouth and bit her knuckles, trying to control a piercing sense of pain. She pulled herself together, the key turned and the door opened. Beth was in the corridor, walking towards her. Dinah's quick glance took in the brief peachy-pink nightshirt Beth was wearing, it came to her thighs and was open at the throat. She looked very young, very pretty and distinctly flushed.

'Oh, hallo, you're home early,' she said and Dinah heard guilt in her tones. 'I wasn't expecting you for hours.'

'Did I wake you up?' Dinah asked her flatly.

'No, I've been revising in bed for hours, I was just thinking of turning out the light and getting to sleep. I thought I'd have some cold milk first.'

'You've been revising all evening?' Dinah said, suppressing her shock and incredulity at the lie. 'All alone? That must have been dull.' She waited for Beth to say something, anything, about Quinn but Beth just laughed, poured herself some milk standing by the fridge in a graceful, unconsciously sexy posture in that brief nightshirt, then wandered to the door, blowing her a kiss.

Dinah sat down abruptly by the kitchen table and stared at her own hands; they shook violently. It was Quinn, then. Why else would Beth pretend to have been here alone all evening? Why else would she lie—and why else would she look as though she had been in heaven all evening?

CHAPTER SIX

She was out of the office for the next few days, filming in Brixton for the second programme in her new series. Most of the interviews were to be done in the street and she didn't want to waste the chance of having good weather, although she watched the burning blue sky with uneasiness because any day now the sweltering heat must break and the rain come. She had had several conversations with local community leaders before she arrived with the camera team and the interviews had all been set up in advance, she wasn't just going to pick at random from the bustling black crowds on Brixton High Street, that way you could waste a lot of film. She couldn't be sure, of course, which of the various people she interviewed would be used for the programme, you could never tell until you saw the footage and realised exactly what you had got. Although people were very vocal off camera the minute they heard the hum which meant the camera was running they clammed up or began to ramble nervously. That was the penalty you paid if you went for vox pop, the public was not professional; on the other hand, when it worked it was terrific, and you only needed one or two good interviews to make the programme work.

Her cameraman was good but waited to be told what to do, he didn't have Patrick's excitement for the work itself. Patrick would have been pointing his camera in all directions; at the run-down Edwardian streets of houses with flaking paintwork, crumbling masonry, boarded-up windows and cluttered gardens full of weeds, torn paper, old beer bottles and crumpled coke cans; at the watermelon smiles of children jigging up and down on the pavements while their mothers gossiped lazily, watching their antics from the broken front steps of houses occupied by half-a-dozen families; at the teenagers in brief, gaudy shorts and sleeveless vests dancing along with their Walkmans clamped over their ears. Patrick would have relished the contrast between the Caribbean weather and the ugly grimness of the streets, it wouldn't have bothered him that he was wasting expensive film which would never be used, he would have been too eager to see and record everything around him. Patrick hated being told what to do, that was why he had gone freelance.

She came home tired and ragged with irritation. Beth was having a bath when Dinah let herself into the flat on the second day of the Brixton interviews; while Dinah was making a pot of tea Beth wandered into the kitchen in a robe, rosy from her bath and very cheerful.

'Hi, had a good day? Isn't this weather fantastic? Do you think it's going to last all summer?'

'I doubt it,' Dinah said and got a surprised look.

'You sound snappy, anything wrong?'

'I'm tired,' Dinah said and walked out. While

she was drinking her tea in the sitting room she heard Beth return to the bedroom. Dinah put on a Bessie Smith record she had bought years ago in a jumble sale; it was scratched and had been played to death but the wry strength of that voice still managed to fill the room. She was choosing music to play under the interviews she had done over the past two days and hadn't made up her mind; she wanted something modern and she meant to use a Bessie Smith recording too, but couldn't decide which.

She threw herself into a chair and lay there, listening, her head back and her eyes closed. Beth must be going out. With Quinn? Dinah forced herself to attend to the song but the poignancy beneath the words made her feel worse. She decided to use a steel band instead, it was obvious, but it was apt.

'I'm going out,' Beth announced from the door, eyeing her uneasily.

Dinah opened her eyes and met that worried look, forcing a smile. 'Okay.' She made no comment, asked no questions. It was none of her business; Quinn wasn't married and he could have no ulterior motive for dating Beth other than a wish to irritate *her*, which was ridiculous, he wouldn't go that far just to needle her. She was getting paranoid, maybe he was right, maybe she was in danger of having a nervous breakdown, her thinking was no longer rational. She had convinced herself that Beth was seeing Max and she had been wrong. Now she was trying to kid herself that Quinn was dating Beth for some tortuous reason when all the time he was

probably dating her because he fancied her. That
was the obvious, the most natural conclusion.
Beth was attractive, she was young and light-
hearted, she was fun.

Beth watched her in a puzzled way. 'What *is*
wrong, Dinah? Something is, I can tell. You
don't seem well, you've been odd for weeks—are
you overworked?'

'You've been talking to Quinn,' Dinah said
with an irony she couldn't resist, and Beth said
too quickly: 'No, I haven't,' then went pink as
Dinah stared at her. Looking at her watch, Beth
muttered: 'I'm going to be late, I must go,' and
was out of the door a second later.

Dinah sat for long minutes staring at nothing
while the silence nagged at her like a tooth with
an exposed nerve. She had had an intimate
acquaintance with pain before; she recognised it
on this second visit, she wanted to shut the door
in its face and she would have done if she had
seen it before it arrived but her unconscious
disguised it from her until too late. When had she
started to feel like this about Quinn? When he
kissed her in Mark's bedroom? Or had it been
there, dormant under the surface of her mind,
seeding quietly and waiting for a warmer climate
before it pushed its way through into the light?
Quinn's angry lovemaking had forced that
growth but she had still refused to see it.

Why had he made love to her like that? Had he
been in that mood? When she rejected him had
he gone back to the party after leaving her at her
flat, and turned his attention to her sister? He
must have gone back to fish for her shoes; if they

had been in the pond all night no amount of polishing and cleaning would have restored them. So Quinn had gone back and Beth had been there; both of them must have been in a similar frame of mind. Beth was looking for someone to help her forget her previous boyfriend, Quinn . . . what had he been looking for? Sex?

Dinah's face burnt, remembering the way he had touched her on the bed, the fierce excitement between them. Had he made love to Beth like that later?

She got up unsteadily and went to have a bath; she couldn't bear to think about it any more. She would eat a light supper and go to bed to work on her ideas for the Brixton programme; she was worried by her lack of invention, her frequent loss of concentration, the weariness which sapped her energy and made idle tears rise to her eyes when she was least expecting them. She had to come up with some new ideas for the next part of the filming; the focus wasn't sharp enough, the ideas strong enough.

When she put out the light at ten-thirty, she told herself as she settled on the pillows in the warm darkness, that the reason why she was so disturbed about Quinn dating her sister was that she was in such a tired state that the least little thing preyed on her mind. She needed a holiday and soon. A fortnight away would make all the difference. She wasn't burnt out or heading for a breakdown, she was just tired. She could cope with her job—demanding though it was—but she couldn't cope with the knowledge that Quinn and the other men were constantly watching her for signs of strain, almost willing her to collapse under the burden of the job. Who wouldn't be tense, feeling all those hostile eyes on them? If she was tired, it was Quinn's fault. He had tried everything he knew to get at her: that lazy mockery, the amused, derisive smiles, the pointed jeers and dry questions, the unceasing undermining of her confidence.

He had even tried the ultimate insult, sex itself; what else was such an uninvited sexual approach but an assault on the identity? He had been reminding her that she was a woman, asserting his masculinity against her, using her own body as an accomplice in his war of attrition, the endless process of wearing her down until she was ready to surrender.

She shut her wet eyes with a shudder of self-reproach—he had got to her, she couldn't deny it, his prophecies had been self-fulfilling, she was caving in, hollow and unable to save herself; Quinn had used emotional voodoo on her. He had told her she was burning out, she needed a long rest, and she was slowly coming to agree with him, but if he had never put the idea into her head would she feel like this? She turned her face into the pillow. She must sleep, she was so tired, and she had another long day ahead of her.

Her dreams were muddled and incoherent; she was filming in Brixton, people talked oddly, she kept stopping them and starting over again, then she was falling into the pond and it wasn't Quinn who pulled her out, it was Max and she melted into his arms, intensely aroused only to find herself standing in the shadows of a tree alone, watching Quinn kissing Beth. She turned and ran away, trembling, and Mark said: 'Isn't it time you talked to her, told her the truth?' She wasn't surprised to be sitting in his office, she just shook her head. 'I can't. I can't.'

She woke up with a jerk of alarm and the flat was filling with pale morning light. Beth was asleep in the bed next to her; she had her back to Dinah, her vivid hair just visible above the bedclothes. Dinah stared across at her, fighting down the odd little feeling niggling in her chest. Had Beth been with Quinn all evening? Were they already lovers? Dinah swung her legs out of bed and crept out of the room; unable to bear the pictures filling her head. In the bathroom she looked at herself in the mirror, her eyes were a savage green. I'm not jealous, she told her reflection. Why on earth should I be? I'm worried, that's all this funny little pain means.

She had a bad day; a running argument with one of the community organisers who had helped her set up the street interviews and some trouble with the camera which held them up for an hour. She was glad to get back to the office later in the afternoon.

'Mark rang, he said he must talk to you the minute you get back,' Angela told her. 'Patrick Forbes rang and said he'd found some fabulous contemporary stills.' She looked up, her eyes curious. 'Oh, and Max Tracy rang twice, he said he'd try your home number tonight.'

Dinah made her face blank. 'Anyone else?' Angela shook her head and Dinah picked up her phone. 'I'd better ring Mark, then.' His secretary answered the second ring and said he was in a meeting, he would ring back.

'Any idea why he wants to talk to me?'

The girl hesitated, and obviously did, but said: 'I'm afraid not, I'll tell him you're back in your office. You'll be there for a while?'

Dinah said yes, rang off and dictated some letters in answer to the mail she had had during the past two days when she wasn't in the office. As Angela went back to her own office, Dinah said: 'Oh, and if Max Tracy rings again, I'm not here. I'm never here when Max Tracy rings.'

Angela made a disbelieving face. 'You must be crazy, he's gorgeous.' She caught Dinah's cold eye and backed out, shrugging, and making no further protest.

Dinah sat at her desk, waiting for Mark to ring, working her way through the photocopied files on Adam Stuart, again looking for anything she might have missed in earlier readings. The foundation of her work was always done in the office, off camera, researching to find a new angle on her subject; her eyes ached with staring at fuzzy print, she was perspiring in the late afternoon heat, her palms clammy. Why didn't that storm break? Everyone was talking about it, waiting for it, but the blue sky was cloudless and the heat intolerable, pressing down on the top of your head as you moved, with waves of hot air hitting you in the face with each step.

The phone rang and she jumped, then snatched it up. 'Hallo?'

'Dinah?'

'Hallo, Mark. You wanted to talk to me?'

'I've had a complaint from one of the local organisations in Brixton,' he began and she groaned, not surprised when Mark told her the name of the man involved.

'Oh, no, what am I supposed to have done?'

'He feels your reporting is biased, you aren't taking his advice, you came down there with a prepared attitude and you only want interviews that fit it. I gather you didn't want to interview him.' Mark sounded wry.

'He wanted to use my programme as a platform. I didn't want politics being aired during the interviews, this was social comment, social reporting, not politics. I did talk to one woman he put up and she was good, I'll use her in the programme, she talked about her life and that was what I wanted.' She gave him a brief sketch of the man who had complained and Mark sighed.

'Did you wrangle with him?'

Dinah flushed. 'We had a little spat—he was trying to dictate the way I made my programme, I wasn't having that.'

Mark was silent for a moment, then he said quietly: 'He's a useful contact. If he turns hostile we may not get any more help from him and he knows people. We can't afford to offend him, you know that.'

'Yes,' she said through her teeth. 'I suppose I was a bit short with him—it was so hot and I was tired and . . . .'

'I see,' Mark said and she became irritable at his tone.

'What do you want me to do? Let him run the show?'

'What harm would there be in doing an interview? You needn't use all of it, just a short snatch, enough to soothe him down.'

'Why should I?' she demanded jaggedly, drumming her fingers on the desk. 'I know what he'd say and it isn't what I'm after—if I decide to do a political programme I'll use him then, he talks a blue streak though, he'll want a lot of film.'

'Have him into the studio tomorrow and give him lunch after you've done a long interview,' Mark said.

'You're kidding. You can't be serious,' she burst out.

'I'm totally serious. Either you give him what he wants or the programme doesn't go out—we can't afford to have a smear campaign running against us. You've got us into a swamp and you're going to have to get us out.'

'I'm damned if I will,' Dinah raged. 'I'm not giving in to blackmail of that sort.'

'Then I'll get Quinn to do it,' Mark said and that was a red rag waved in her face, she almost shouted back at him. 'You will not! Quinn Howard isn't getting his hands on my programme. Is he behind this? It's some sort of conspiracy is it?' She no longer knew what she was saying, her anger burst the banks and flooded everything in sight, she heard the door open and Angela stared across the office at her with a shocked face, and only then did she realise how loudly she was shouting. She stopped dead, swallowing, going white, hearing Mark breathing on the other end of the line.

After a long silence he said curtly: 'I'm coming

down. Stay there.' The phone slammed down and she held her own end, trembling violently. What had she said to him? She didn't even know, she couldn't remember, her mind was a complete blank.

'What's happened?' Angela asked breathlessly.

'I don't know,' Dinah let her head drop into her hands because she couldn't bear anyone to see her face. She had talked at Mark blindly, but what had she said? Crazy, angry things; his mention of Quinn had been the last straw, her irritation over the complaint had been nothing to the rage she had felt when Mark threatened to give her programme to Quinn, the top of her head had seemed to blow off and she had spilled out the bitterness she had felt for too long. Words had poured out of her like molten metal. Mark was going to be furious; how could he forget what she had said? How could she have talked to him like that?

Outside she heard a deep distant rumble of thunder; the storm was approaching at last. The sky was darkening, there was a flash of lightning and Angela jumped.

'Oh!' She moved backward to the door. 'Can I get you some coffee?'

'Thank you,' Dinah said listlessly, wondering what Mark would say when he got here.

Angela went out and was back in a short while with a paper cup of black coffee from the machine. Dinah fumbled for some money and Angela took it, lingering. 'Can I do anything? I mean, aren't you well? Headache? I've got some asprin.'

'Just leave me alone,' Dinah said irritably as the sky flashed again and the thunder growled a moment later. How close was the storm? When would it break overhead? Angela went out, closing the door with a bang. Now Dinah had offended her. This was definitely not her day; she had been snarling at everyone since she started work in the overheated streets whose pavements sweated as she walked on them.

She drank some of the coffee; it tasted bitter. She put down the cup and the door opened and Mark looked at her across the room, frowning, his face stern.

'I'm sorry,' Dinah said. 'I'm sorry, Mark. I don't know what I ... I'm sorry.' She put her head down again and began to cry harshly, shuddering, her body shaking as the sobs wrenched out of her.

Mark came over and pulled her up out of the chair, held her close, patting her heaving shoulders.

Through gulped sobs she said: 'I'm too hot and tired, it's been a hell of a day, my head aches and I hate thunderstorms, the pressure has been building up and up, it just blew, I'm sorry it was you who got it.'

Mark listened and said nothing. When she had cried herself out she stood with her head on his chest, afraid to let him see her face. His shirt was wet as her cheek brushed it, she had cried all over him.

'I'll drive you home,' Mark said at last.

'No, there's no need, I'm okay,' she protested and he pushed her away and looked at her calmly, his face unreadable.

'Get your things, we're going now.'

She was afraid he was going to sack her, take her programme away from her, she tried to read that shuttered face but he wasn't giving anything away. Mark was a born diplomat, when he chose to exercise his skill you couldn't get past his blank mask. Dinah's hands dropped to her side, she nodded wearily, accepting it. She had no choice.

'Beth won't be at home now,' he murmured as she gathered up her bag and a pile of notes on her series. 'You should have someone with you—would you like Angela to. . . .'

'No,' she said fiercely. 'I'm not crazy, I don't need a nurse, I'm just tired. I'll get a good night's sleep and I'll be fine tomorrow.'

'I'll try to get hold of Beth,' Mark thought aloud and she frowned.

'She may be anywhere in the college—the library, a lecture room. And I don't need her, it's ridiculous, I won't have a fuss made.'

'Okay,' Mark said soothingly and guided her out of the office, across the landing and into the lift. Dinah was still shaky, she had to lean on the wall because her legs were too weak to support her. Mark watched her and she wished he wouldn't; she kept her eyes down. 'I am sorry, Mark,' she said.

'Never mind that now, you're not well,' he said and she hated what she suspected was going on inside his head. Was he working out who to put in charge of her programme? Well, she knew who that would be, didn't she? He had been waiting long enough, his day was here, wasn't he lucky?

'Don't let Quinn. . . .' she began but where was the point of saying it? Mark was going to make the decision whatever she said; she had destroyed her own credibility, she had screamed at him on the phone like some demented creature and he wasn't going to listen to her now.

She walked across the car park beside Mark and waited while he unlocked his car and stood back to let her climb into the passenger seat. He walked around the back of the car then paused, looking back. Dinah heard the hurried footsteps on the tarmac, she looked in the wing mirror and saw a distorted image of Quinn running towards them. She heard Mark speak to him, they moved out of earshot, murmuring to each other. Dinah closed her eyes, shivering as if she had flu.

She might not be able to hear what they were saying, but she could guess. Quinn was questioning Mark—had he already heard on the grapevine that she had gone crazy, insulting Mark, screaming at him? They didn't lose any time. It must have been Angela, she must have dashed out to tell her friends who would have been on the phone to other people as soon as she had left. News travelled fast in a big office block; it would have multiplied, swelled to exaggerated size by now. Anyone hearing the gossip at this moment was probably being told that she had run mad and smashed all the furniture, cut Mark's throat and danced naked in the studio, had sex with three cameramen and burnt all her film on a bonfire in the street. The truth was too tame for them, they fed on real life drama and had a lurid taste for soap opera which her dull little explosion of rage wouldn't satisfy.

Quinn was no doubt getting Mark's go ahead to take over *One Nation*. She had done most of the paper groundwork; he wouldn't have much trouble picking up from where she had left off. He couldn't even wait for Mark to get back, could he?

She felt too weary and dull to care any more. She slumped in the seat with her closed eyes aware of the flashes of lightning coming closer and closer. The door opened and Mark got into the driver's seat. The engine started and the car backed and began to move off. Dinah opened her eyes and lightning flashed in her iris, she blinked, jerking with nerves. The storm was almost overhead now. The sky was black. She turned her head and saw the long-fingered hands on the wheel, then looked with dazed shock from them to the face of the man beside her.

Quinn turned his black head and stared at her with cool penetration. She ran her tongue over her dry lips, hardly able to speak.

'Where's Mark gone?'

'He was wanted urgently back in his office. I'm driving you home instead.'

A flare of panic lit the greyness around her. She turned and put a hand on the door handle. 'I'll take a taxi!'

'Don't be stupid.' He put on speed, his hand grasping her arm at the same time, holding her in her seat.

She saw big spots of rain spreading on the windscreen and stared at them dully, slackening in the seat. Quinn's hand released her, he put it back on the wheel. The rain fell in silvery sheets, turning the streets into fast-running rivers within minutes, the pavements were black, people dived into shop doorways and leapt on buses. Suddenly the busy London streets were empty except for a few hurrying figures holding newspapers over their heads in a hopeless way. Thunder crashed and reverberated, lightning split the dark sky. Quinn slowed, his tyres shrieking on the wet road.

Dinah was crying. She didn't know why. She didn't make a sound, the tears just slid down her face and she stared at the windscreen seeing it blurred. Quinn pushed a handkerchief into her hand and she put it dumbly over her face, hiding behind it until the tears stopped leaking from her lids and she could dry her face and blow her nose. By then they had reached her flat and Quinn peered out at the tumbling rain, grim-faced.

'We'll get soaked.'

'You stay here, I'll run for it,' she muttered.

Quinn took off his jacket and pushed it at her. 'Put this over your head, it will keep some of the rain off.'

She got out and ran, huddled under his jacket, feeling water splashing on her legs and into her shoes. The path was puddled with rain, great bubbles formed on the surface of the pools and burst with a little splash. She kept her eyes down but she knew Quinn was on her heels. They arrived in the doorway together.

She lowered his jacket and handed it to him. 'Thank you, I'll be okay now.'

'Got your key?'

She nodded and walked away. He followed so she muttered huskily: 'There's no need to see me into my flat, you know.' She got out her key and found the lock. As the door swung open she hurried inside but not fast enough, Quinn was still on her heels. Dinah turned and looked up at him, scowling.

'Please, I want you to go, I don't need company, especially. . . .'

'Mine?' he asked when her voice trailed off and she mutely nodded. 'Well, that's too bad, because I'm staying here until Mark finds your sister.'

Colour poured up her face, her lips trembled. Quinn stared at her in blank amazement, as she burst out: 'Oh, *you* know where she is, do you? Did she give you her timetable so that you could find her whenever you wanted her?'

'What the hell are you talking about?' Quinn was frowning, his black brows a jagged slash across his forehead.

'Some secrets can't be kept. I'm not as dumb as you think. I know you're dating Beth—I don't know what all the secrecy's about. Beth's old enough to do as she likes. I may think she must be crazy to want to date you but I couldn't stop her and I wouldn't even try.'

He kept his hard eyes fixed on her as she talked in a rapid, impeded voice; his face was very still now and Dinah felt afraid of the harsh constriction of his jawline. She backed away, her eyes alarmed, yet still bitterly angry with him, and Quinn moved towards her. The lightning seemed to have got inside his eyes, they flashed violently at her and Dinah grew icy cold.

CHAPTER SEVEN

'WHERE did you get that crazy idea?' he asked through tight lips and Dinah tried to look away from those blindingly angry eyes but was transfixed by them, could not look away.

'Don't try to lie to me. I saw you here the other night. You came out and got into your car and don't tell me you just happened to drop in casually because it was midnight and nobody just drops round at that time of night.'

'A few nights ago?' he said, still staring at her. 'Yes, I came round here very late at night but I didn't go into your flat or even see your sister—I was delivering a book. I'd intended to bring it round earlier in the evening. I was having dinner with some friends half a mile away from here and I promised to drop a book off for Beth but I forgot, it just slipped my mind. Halfway through dinner I remembered it, so on my way home I stopped and ran up to your flat to push the book through the letterbox.' He sounded so calm that Dinah was confused and uncertain.

'Why are you lending her books if you aren't seeing her?' she demanded, seeing the flaw in his denial. He had answered her specific point but he hadn't really said pointblank that he was not dating Beth; typical of him to try to hoodwink her with a devious piece of mental sleight of hand.

'I'm not lending her books. I was delivering one, I was just a messenger.'

'Who did. . . .' she broke off, frowning, rubbing a hand across her head. She couldn't think clearly but they seemed to be getting off the point.

'That's a question you must ask your sister,' Quinn said flatly. 'Why don't you go to bed? You look terrible.' His eyes assessed the pallor of her face.

She felt even worse as he said that, hypersensitive at that moment to everything he said and every look he gave her. 'You can't stay here,' was all she said though. 'I don't need a babysitter and I'm not going to bed while you're in my flat.'

'Never?' he asked with cool mockery and her colour came back in a scalding flood.

'What do you want—a harem? Isn't Beth enough for you? Do you have to flirt with me too?'

She saw the anger in his eyes again and flinched. Quinn took her arm and pushed her down the corridor towards the bedroom, talking curtly. 'Go to bed.'

She wrenched herself free, facing him with feverish eyes. 'Don't give me orders! Go back to Metro and get on with taking over my programme—that's what you've wanted all along, why you've been prodding and needling me for months. Well, now you've got what you want, why are you hanging around here? Getting some kick out of gloating over me? Do you want to see what you've done to me?'

'You've done it to yourself,' Quinn said in a hard, cold voice.

'Like hell I have!'

'I warned you,' Quinn said, making her even angrier.

'Oh, yes—you warned me. You're so damned clever, chanting your prophecies in my ear day after day until you made me so frantic they came true. You conditioned me to crack up, I was fine until you came along, with those black magic eyes and. . . .'

'So now it's my fault,' Quinn said in a weary way.

'You bet it is!'

'I suppose you have to blame someone—anything rather than face the truth. It couldn't be overwork. You're superhuman, aren't you? You've convinced yourself that you have to be tougher and better than anyone else and you won't admit that you're made of the same stuff as the rest of humanity.'

'You mean I'm not up to it because I'm a woman!' she accused and he made an impatient gesture.

'*You're* obsessed with that, I'm not. Everyone needs to take it easy once in a while—whatever their sex—but not you. You push yourself to the limit, don't you?' He looked at her oddly, his mouth indenting, she heard him give a faint sigh. 'You've got guts, I admit; I admire your tenacity and courage, but you're living on a knife edge all the time, Dinah. You never relax and enjoy life, you've lost any sense of humour you ever had, your temper is hair-trigger and irrational.'

She leaned against the wall because she was afraid she might actually pass out if she didn't have some support. Outside the storm was still raging; the vivid flash of lightning occasionally lit the dimness of the corridor and the deep roll of thunder answered like a threatening voice. She couldn't think clearly.

'I blew up when I was talking to Mark,' she thought aloud. 'He told you, I suppose. Everyone will know about it by now.'

He didn't deny it, he was watching her intently. 'Do you know *why* you can't relax? That would use up energy you need for your job and you can't risk that. If you're going to stay ahead you have to keep running—that's what you think, isn't it? But don't you see? By using up your energy without ever taking time off to recharge your batteries, you're driving yourself into the ground. You're defeating yourself.'

'I'm tired,' she said through cold, weary lips and it was an effort just to say it; yet at the same time it was a relief and she knew she had been feeling tired for weeks but had pushed the admission to the very furthest recesses of her mind. She had had to concentrate on planning her next series; she couldn't allow herself to feel tired.

Quinn picked her up in one sudden movement and she clutched at his shoulders in alarm as her feet left the ground. He gave her a brief smile and carried her down the corridor, and Dinah was too tired to fight him or struggle to get down, she let her head fall on his shoulder and her body seemed so heavy that she wondered how he managed to carry her with such apparent lack of effort. He pushed the bedroom door open and carried her across the room to the bed.

Dinah sighed as the mattress gave beneath her weight, she lay quiescent with closed eyes, longing to get to sleep. Quinn sat beside her and she didn't bother to open her eyes, it was comforting to have him there and she didn't have any more energy to fight him with. The room was quiet except for the continuing storm which was diminishing, moving away across the rain-swept city like some growling, spitting animal receding into the distance.

Quinn's hand touched her shirt; he was unbuttoning it and Dinah made no protest. The movements of his fingers had a strangely soothing sensuality. If she didn't move or open her eyes she could stay within this dreamlike mood, free of guilt or self-contempt, initiating nothing but silently accepting the gentle brush of his fingertips over her naked breast. Quinn slid a hand round the back of her neck and she felt him raise her, he pulled her shirt off and dropped it with the bra he had already removed. Her nape was tense with the day's problems, Quinn firmly kneaded it with that long-fingered hand and her taut muscles eased, making her sigh with pleasure. His clasp moved down to her shoulders, massaging them in the same way, then he ran his hand down the bare spine of her back and she felt the tiny hairs along that deep indentation bristle with excitement. He unzipped her skirt and eased it off; she felt him staring at her slender, relaxed body, and her mind drowned in a confused wash of desire and troubled uncertainty.

She despised herself for giving in to her craving for this sensual comfort, she was a weak fool, she shouldn't have let him go this far—had she forgotten Beth? She knew she hadn't, she was deliberately suppressing the memory of her sister, and she was ashamed of herself. She forced her eyes open and met Quinn's darkened eyes with a stab of pain, then grabbed the edge of the quilt she was lying on and rolled it over herself until she was covered from neck to foot. Silently, Quinn sat back with his arms folded and a watchful expression on his face.

'What if Beth walked in? What lies would you tell her?' Dinah accused, her gaze lowered because she did not want him to read anything in her eyes, she had not wanted to stop him and it might show in her face.

'I wouldn't need to tell her any lies,' he said tersely. He ran a hand over his thick black hair, she heard him breathing impatiently. 'Look, I am not dating your sister—I don't know how you got the idea I was, it's all part of what's wrong with you, I suppose, you just aren't thinking rationally. If I was dating Beth, I wouldn't be secretive about it—why should I? She's of age, she's free to go out with anyone she chooses.'

His voice carried conviction, Dinah's eyes lifted to his face and she searched it in silence for a moment, frowning.

'She's going out with someone, I'm certain of it—and she doesn't want me to know, she's being very secretive.' Her head turned on the pillow, she stared at the window and saw a distant flash of lightning, her eyes leapt with surprise at it. 'Who can it be, then. . . .' Had she been right first time? Had it been Max?

'Isn't her private life her own affair?' Quinn asked drily. 'If she doesn't want to talk about it why ferret away trying to guess?'

'I don't want her to get hurt!'

'The way you were?' he probed coolly and she flushed.

When she didn't answer, Quinn said curtly: 'Max Tracy may have been a cheat and a liar, that doesn't mean every man you meet is tarred with the same brush.'

'Not every man, maybe—but a lot of them are, they use the women they meet for one reason or another; sometimes it's just sexual, they treat women like disposable hankies, use them once and then chuck them away. Sometimes it's more subtle, they want something more than sex. With Max it was a chance to meet useful people. Once I'd introduced him to everyone useful I knew, he was finished with me, he couldn't get any more out of me.' She stopped and looked at him and he read the expression in her angry eyes and frowned.

'And me?' he prompted. 'I was next on your list, wasn't I?'

'You know what *you* want,' she said, looking away because it hurt to remember his real reason for being interested in her. While those sensitive fingertips of his had been caressing her body it had been so easy to forget, to hoodwink herself that Quinn wanted her for the oldest, most basic reason in the world. She hadn't needed then to ask if he was in love with her—she had only wanted to surrender to the aching torment which his touch had aroused inside her, nothing else had seemed to matter for a few minutes.

'Yes,' he replied drily. 'But do you?'

'I'm not that dumb. You've made it blazingly obvious!'

'I thought so,' he agreed in the same dry voice. 'But you showed no sign of getting my message.'

She was bewildered, meeting his derisive eyes with uncertainty. 'You want to take over my programme, you want me out of Metro.' She half wanted him to deny it, to tell her she had misread his attitude. She didn't know if she would believe him but she couldn't help wishing she had been totally wrong about him, she was tired of their clashes and enmity, she wanted peace at almost any price at this moment.

He stroked a bright strand of hair back from her cheek, smiling. 'Forget about work, this is personal. It's a different game.'

'Is it?' she whispered, hypnotised again by the brush of his fingers and knowing that every pore in her skin was aware of his touch.

'It's time you learnt to play more and work less. Everyone should be a game player; there's no better way to relax and you'll be amazed how much you learn while you're having fun. Look at the way baby animals behave; they're playing at what they'll do for real when they are fully mature. I have a strong suspicion you missed out on that phase; you got your fingers burnt over Max Tracy and wouldn't play any more. You took him too seriously; you take everything too seriously, including your work.' His blue eyes mocked her gently.

'You see love as a game?' she asked with a faint chill of disappointment and Quinn laughed.

'Love games can turn serious, but first you have to agree to play at all.'

'And risk getting burnt?' Dinah said flatly.

'Everything's a risk,' Quinn said watching her with attentive eyes that made her self-conscious. 'But especially human beings because they're more unpredictable than anything else in the world, they don't conform to patterns and they aren't always sure about their own motives.'

'They're deceptive, too,' she said, thinking of Max.

'We're not going to argue in one of your vicious circles, are we? You're too tired to talk, you should be resting. Where's your nightie?' He stood up and glanced around, saw her nightdress case at the foot of the bed and pulled the cotton nightie out of it, tossing it to her. 'I'll wait until your sister gets here. Is there anything you want? A drink? Something to eat?'

She was taken aback by the abrupt change of mood and mutely shook her head. Quinn puzzled her, she didn't know what to make of him. What had he really been talking about? Had she read something more personal into his talk of love games and relaxing than had actually been there?

He considered her, his head to one side. 'My mother's first reaction to a crisis is always to make a pot of tea. Why don't I do that?' He didn't wait for an answer, he went out, closing the door behind him. Dinah pulled the nightie over her head with unsteady hands and climbed between the sheets, folding back the quilt which was far too heavy for weather as hot as this. She subsided against her pillows and watched the sky, drifts of dark clouds rolling away to reveal the fathomless blue behind them. She was lost in thought, her face bewildered. If Beth wasn't dating Quinn why was she being so secretive? She knew she was deeply relieved to find out that the man in Beth's life wasn't Quinn; that would have been disastrous. What if it had been serious? What if Beth had married him? Dinah closed her eyes with a painful sigh; unable to bear the idea of Quinn becoming her brother-in-law.

The door opened suddenly and she opened her eyes, instantly agitated, as though he might read her thoughts in her face, but it wasn't Quinn coming into the room—it was Beth, looking worried.

'I'm sorry they bothered you,' Dinah said apologetically. 'There's really nothing much wrong with me—just too much heat and too much hassle.'

Beth came over to kiss her and sat down on the bed, studying her soberly. 'You don't look well, though, you haven't for days—Mark thinks you ought to see a doctor. Why don't I call ours and ask him to come round?'

'No,' Dinah said. 'You know what he'd say— I'm overworked and depressed. Then he'd write me out a prescription for Valium or something like that, tell me to have a holiday or take up golf and he'd leave whistling. He can't tell me anything I can't work out for myself and I don't want to start taking tranquillisers, thank you!'

There was a tap at the door and Quinn came in

carrying a tray on which was arranged two cups and saucers, a teapot and milk jug and sugar bowl. He lowered it to her bedside table. 'Shall I pour it for you? Milk? Sugar?'

Beth grinned at him. 'That's what we've always needed—a home help. You've got the job.'

Quinn laughed, pouring the tea. Dinah watched his appreciative glance at Beth's triangular little face, her vivid hair and the slender neatness of her figure in the green cotton dungarees and short-sleeved yellow T-shirt. Beth was very decorative and brimming with life. She made Dinah feel more tired than ever.

'Isn't it time you asked Beth that question?' Quinn prodded and her gaze flew to his face, startled.

'What question?' Beth enquired, taking her cup from him.

'Shut up,' Dinah muttered, suddenly realising what he meant.

'Your sister was under the impression you were having a secret affair with me,' he told Beth in a drawling tone.

'I didn't say that!' Dinah was bright red.

Beth stared at her, open-mouthed. 'Dinah! You thought . . . me and Quinn . . . how on earth could you think that? What a crazy idea!'

'Well, thank you,' Quinn said and she giggled.

'Sorry, Quinn, I only meant that you'd be the last man in . . . oops! I'd better start again.' She put a hand over her mouth, shaking with embarrassed laughter.

'You're not exactly doing wonders for my ego,' he agreed, one fine black brow curved perfectly in wry resignation. 'Dinah saw me deliver that book the other night and jumped to the conclusion that I had been with you all evening— and I don't think she suspected that we had been studying literature.'

'Why don't you go back to the office?' Dinah said through her teeth. Beth was flushed and agitated and Quinn gave her a quick glance, shrugging.

'I suppose I'd better. Don't let her get out of that bed, Beth. Use force if you have to, but make her stay put for a couple of days and try to get her to take a holiday. She's a stubborn idiot but Mark would hate it if Metro lost her.'

The door closed behind him and Dinah lay, listening to the sound of his footsteps walking out of earshot.

He's gorgeous, isn't he?' Beth said a little too brightly and Dinah looked at her quickly. Her lips parted but she didn't say what she had been going to say because she suddenly realised what it would have been. He's mine, she had been going to tell Beth, she had felt a stab of jealousy as Beth talked about him. I'm out of my mind, she thought. Maybe he's right. Maybe I am going crazy, I must be to think that Quinn belongs to me. But she hadn't been thinking—that was the whole trouble. Sheer instinctive reaction had put the words on the tip of her tongue; it had been her mind that froze them there. Am I turning schizoid? Her intelligence saw Quinn one way—her feelings saw him very differently. That split was worrying, Dinah lay back on her pillow and worried, chewing her lip, forgetting her sister for a moment.

'You didn't seriously think that I was making it with Quinn, did you?' Beth asked and Dinah looked at her with violent green eyes. Beth jumped back in alarm. 'I've only met him once,' she protested. 'Until today. Honestly—he put a book through the letterbox that night, that's all.' Her flush grew hectic. She looked down, lacing her fingers on her knee. 'Mark lent it to me, I needed it for an essay I was working on and I couldn't get a copy from the library, they were all out to other people. Mark couldn't bring it round because he was going to some important dinner so he asked Quinn to drop it in on his way somewhere else.'

'I know, he explained. I'm sorry I jumped to conclusions but you've been so secretive about your new boyfriend and it occurred to me that if it was Quinn you might not want to tell me because you know that Quinn's at daggers drawn with me in the office.'

Beth gave her a strange look, she was grinning oddly. 'Come off it! You fancy him, you know you do.'

Dinah went red. 'Who says?'

'I've got eyes, I can see, whenever you're with him you could cut the atmosphere with a knife.'

Dinah sat upright, hurriedly dragging a dignified incredulity into her face. 'Don't be ridiculous.' She looked at the teapot. 'I'd like another cup of tea, will you pour it?'

Beth laughed infuriatingly. 'Okay. Change of subject.' She poured some tea, grimacing. 'It's lukewarm—shall I make some more?'

'No, that will do.' Dinah didn't really want any

tea anyway, she nursed the cup and sipped some of the warm liquid, her eyes lowered. 'Beth, it isn't Max Tracy you're seeing, is it?'

'No, it isn't,' Beth said emphatically. 'Do you have to know? I mean, can't you wait until I'm ready to talk about him?'

'It's just that there's something you ought to know about Max Tracy,' Dinah said huskily, nerving herself to tell her sister the whole story. She swallowed on a hard lump in her throat, then plunged into rapid, low sentences. Beth sat still on the bed, watching her and listening without interruption, although once or twice Dinah felt her shift as though she wanted to say something.

'So you see why I'm wary about men's motives,' Dinah ended grimly. 'I'm not just being conventional when I give you a gypsy's warning about being careful with them.'

'What a rat!' Beth breathed. 'I wish I'd known—I'd have kicked his shins when I met him at the party. Mind you, I thought he was a bit of a fake—those very good-looking men often are, aren't they? They're too busy thinking how wonderful they are to have time to think about anyone else. I told you what Gary was like—he was a Max Tracy; he felt it was his duty to the opposite sex to put himself about as much as possible. I felt a fool when I worked that out. You do, don't you? You could scream when you realise you've been had. Mark says that he suspects anyone who never makes a mistake, though. It means they're either lying or they just aren't human.'

Dinah stared at her, a sudden blinding thought

hitting her between the eyes. 'You keep quoting Mark,' she said slowly and hot colour surged up Beth's face. 'Have you seen him since the party?' She read the answer in her sister's lowered eyes, the agitated shifting of her fingers. 'Beth, is it . . . it can't be! Mark's old enough . . . .'

'To be my father,' Beth supplied crossly. 'I know. He keeps pointing it out. I knew you wouldn't approve, so did he. There's nothing you can say that Mark hasn't already said to me, I know all the arguments.'

Dinah put down her cup, her hand shaking so much it made the cup rattle in the saucer. 'Beth, he's been married before—he's got a son not so many years younger than you!'

'I've met him. We got on fine. He didn't seem to mind his Dad going out with me.'

Dinah sat in silence, angry with Mark, too taken aback to know what to say to her sister. What on earth would their parents say when they discovered that Beth was dating a man who was twice her age? Mark was forty; he was very sophisticated and experienced, he could be tougher than Quinn and he was used to having his own way. Any relationship he had with Beth must be unequal, balanced in Mark's favour, it had been unfair of him to start dating her. No wonder he had kept it a secret.

'Mark feels guilty because I'm so much younger,' Beth said. 'He goes through a big performance every time he takes me out—asking me if I'm sure I won't be bored, isn't there someone closer to my own age I'd rather be with, doing silly arithmetic all the time. When I'm thirty he'll be over fifty, that sort of thing. He's afraid people will say he's cradle-snatching.'

'Well, isn't he?'

Beth stood up, flushed and angry. 'No, he isn't. Any snatching that was done was done by me.'

Dinah laughed disbelievingly. 'Oh, Beth, really!'

'It's true. Mark didn't ask me out in the first place. I asked him.' Beth met her eyes, defiance in her face. 'I did, I don't mind admitting it. Why shouldn't I? You've drummed it into me for years that women are equal to men. When I danced with Mark at his party I knew I liked him more than anyone I've ever met. He told me he was a terrific Mozart freak and I knew there was going to be a Mozart concert at the college that week. I hadn't meant to go but I asked Mark if he'd like to go with me.' She laughed abruptly, her face changing. 'He was a bit taken aback but he said he'd like to come and it was a marvellous evening. As it was my idea I took him out to supper afterwards, we went to a MacDonalds, I told him it was all I could afford on my grant and he laughed and said: next time it's on me—so I said: okay, name a day.'

'Beth!' Dinah said, staggered.

Beth looked aggressively at her. 'What? Look, I could tell Mark liked me but he's as conventional as you are—he didn't think he ought to do what I could tell he wanted to do. We had had a great time together, I loved every minute of it and I was sure he felt the same.'

'Nevertheless,' Dinah said hesitantly and Beth grimaced at her.

'Mark isn't shy, if he didn't want to see me he wouldn't be slow in making it clear. I'm not pushing myself at a reluctant guy, I'm giving the green light to a man who likes me a lot but needs persuasion because of outdated ideas about an age gap.'

Dinah thought back over the past few weeks of euphoria and depression. Her face disturbed she asked: 'Are you in love with him, Beth?'

'I think he's wonderful,' Beth said, glowing, then she sobered and gave a sigh. 'I don't want to make it so definite, don't you see? I'd scare Mark off, I might even scare myself off. I'm waiting to see, I don't want to hurry anything. That's why I didn't tell you; I don't want anyone to interfere or try to influence Mark. This is our decision, our lives. I don't care what anyone else thinks.'

Dinah lay looking at her, very worried. Beth took her cup, put it on the tray and carried the tray to the door. 'You'd better get some sleep now. Mark's very worried about you, I promised I'd take care of you and make sure you didn't try to work. Are you sure you won't see a doctor? Don't you think you should?'

Dinah turned on to her side, pulling the sheet over her head, and Beth gave a grunt of amusement. 'Well, have it your way,' she said and went out.

Dinah didn't expect to sleep now, her mind was too busy with the new ideas Beth had given it to work on, but as the sky darkened towards night she slowly fell asleep and only woke when sunlight troubled her lids, making her open her eyes and blink in the dazzle of morning. She looked at the clock on her bedside table. It was nearly ten o'clock, she had slept for more than twelve hours.

She got up, went to the bathroom, sleepily inspected her flushed face in the mirror, then went padding along the corridor to the kitchen, expecting to find Beth there.

The flat was empty, however. Beth had left a note on the table. Dinah read it, smiling. Beth had slipped out to do some shopping and would be back soon, Dinah was not to get dressed or go anywhere or *else*! Putting on the kettle, Dinah spooned instant coffee into a mug then made herself some toast. She sat down five minutes later with her breakfast, skimming the morning paper as she bit into the crisp brown toast spread thinly with marmalade. She hadn't eaten breakfast for years, she normally made do with coffee and perhaps an orange.

The window was open, a light breeze blew through her hair. She felt calmer today; the incredible pressure and tension of yesterday morning had gone while she slept and she winced as she remembered her eruption on the phone to Mark, wishing she could live yesterday all over again. She had been a complete fool; over so many things—she shouldn't have been pushing herself so hard, she shouldn't have let her mind leap to so many crazy conclusions about Beth and her secret boyfriend, she shouldn't have let her temper fray at the edges over tiny things that really didn't matter. But it was too late to realise all that. Mark was going to be having second thoughts about her stability, somehow she had to convince him that she wasn't going to get into that state again. She would take a few days off and in the meantime hope Mark didn't hand her series over to anyone else. He wouldn't move too fast. Surely he would wait and see how she was when she had had a holiday? All she had to do was get well enough to do the Adam Stuart interview—that was the first programme which would be going out. She had more than a week. She felt so much better today she knew she would be fighting fit again in time to do that interview.

When the doorbell rang she smiled, getting up. Beth had forgotten her key again, she was always doing it. Dinah pulled open the front door, amusement in her face, and stared in surprise at Max Tracy.

'Hallo, Dinah,' he said, giving her that charming smile which he produced with the ease of a conjuror pulling rabbits from a hat. She barred his way, impatiently conscious of the way he was looking over the peach-coloured négligé which matched the cotton nightdress she wore under it.

'What do you want, Max? I'm having a rest day, I really can't talk to anyone.'

'I brought you these,' he said, pulling a large bunch of flowers from behind his back. 'I wondered if you could have dinner again tonight? Or on Saturday?'

She reluctantly took the flowers. 'Thank you but I'm afraid I'm not free, tonight or Saturday.'

'Is that when you're doing the Adam Stuart programme?' Max asked and she suddenly caught the urgency under his casual tone and looked at him with sharp interest. She stepped back, clutching the flowers.

'Come in while I put these in water,' she said, and Max followed her into the kitchen and watched her fill a large vase with water and begin arranging the flowers in it. Dinah was thinking hard; she didn't want to rush to any more wild conclusions, she might have read Max's tone wrongly but she was curious, she wanted to know why he was pursuing her with such insistence.

'I'm not doing the Stuart programme until next week,' she said lightly, inhaling the spicy scent of red carnations while she slid them one by one into the vase. 'Do you know him, Max?'

'No, we've never met,' Max said and she was certain he was speaking warily.

'He's too busy finalising the casting for his film,' Dinah said and shot him a quick glance from under her lashes. Max was staring at her slim fingers as they stripped some leaves from a flower stem. He was looking totally blank, and that was interesting in itself since Max was always acting, he was never genuine—that blank expression hid something.

'He's doing that this week?' he asked in a flat, unreadable tone.

Dinah turned and stared openly at him. 'What are you after, Max? A chance to meet Adam Stuart? Do you want a part in his film?'

He flushed and stared back at her; she sensed that he was weighing up several answers, trying to work out the best way of replying.

'For once in your life tell the truth,' Dinah said with impatient humour, smiling at him. 'It won't do you any good to lie, not this time. Do you want to meet Adam Stuart?'

He said: 'Yes,' with a placating grin, acting wry self-reproach. 'Well, you can't blame me, darling—it would be such a terrific chance, a good part in that film, but he's hedged in behind the money men and his entourage, nobody can get near him. I know he'd like me if he met me. I'm not expecting a starring part—but I happen to know there is one part that would be perfect for me but there are others after it.' He stopped, giving her a pleading smile. 'That wasn't my only reason for wanting to see you, honestly, Dinah, I have missed you and I like you a lot.' He moved and caught her arms, smiling down at her. 'You really are terrific.' He bent his head to kiss her and she felt a qualm of curiosity—would it mean anything to her now? When she saw him at Mark's party she had been violently angry and rather scared; she had loved him so much once, did she still care? She hadn't admitted it to herself then but she had wondered if the odd emotions churning around inside her were love or contempt. She was sure Max left her cold now, but she decided to make quite certain. She lifted her lips and Max kissed her with an expert awareness of what he was doing; he injected passion into that kiss and Dinah didn't feel a thing.

She had her eyes shut, she was concentrating on her own reactions so hard she didn't hear the front door opening, but when Beth giggled in the doorway Dinah and Max leapt apart. Max self-consciously smoothed his hair, looking round.

Dinah stiffened, staring at Quinn's hard face as he eyed her over Beth's shoulder.

'Oops, sorry,' Beth said, giving Dinah a disbelieving, enquiring look, which was not surprising after everything Dinah had told her about Max. 'Shall we go out and come in again?'

Max pretended to laugh. 'I was just on my way,' he said, moving to the door. Beth and Quinn cleared a path for him, he seemed uneasy under their stare, or was it only Quinn's icy eyes that bothered him? Dinah felt oddly sorry for him, he must be the most pathetic creature I've ever met, she thought. She would hate to go to the lengths Max went to in his pursuit of fame, she would feel diminished, shabby, very sick of herself. Max obviously found it possible to live with himself, of course, but Dinah impulsively said after him: 'I'll see what I can do about Adam Stuart.'

Max stopped dead and looked round at her, flushing. She smiled wryly at him and he gave an almost shy smile back.

'I'll ring you,' she said. 'I'll talk to Mark—maybe we could have a voice-over on this programme, if you're free to do it.'

'Yes,' Max said eagerly. 'I'd love to.' He paused. 'Thanks, Dinah.'

Quinn closed the door after him; it slammed so hard that she thought the glass in the windows would break. Quinn turned and looked at her with contempt and cold anger.

Beth looked from his face to Dinah's and tactfully melted out of sight into the bedroom.

CHAPTER EIGHT

'DON'T you ever learn?' Quinn asked in a voice which breathed pure rage. Dinah ignored him, picking up the vase of flowers and carrying it into the sitting room. She walked past him without so much as a glance and Quinn followed her.

'No answer?' he jeered. 'You don't like to admit what a fool you are, I suppose.'

'Does anyone?' Dinah enquired, placing the vase on a table and standing back to admire the effect, aware that Quinn watched her but pretending total indifference.

'You know what sort of guy he is!' he said impatiently.

'Better than you do!'

'Oh, you think you can reform him, I suppose?' Quinn grated. 'You're crazy, he'll make you unhappy.' He took a deep breath. 'Are you in love with him?'

Dinah looked round at the force in his voice and saw his hands clenched at his sides as though to prevent him using them violently. There was no mockery or amusement in his lean face now; it held a ráw anger that frightened her and yet she bristled with offence at the contempt in those blue eyes. He had no right to look at her like that—she could tell him that she wasn't stupid, she wouldn't make a fool of herself over Max again, but the way Quinn was staring at her made her angry in return, she did not like the scathing assumption behind his rage. It was all part of his basic attitude to women; he despised them, even the comforting concern he had shown her when she was ill had sprung from the same source. Quinn saw her sex as emotional, irrational creatures less able to cope with life than men. He had no respect for women on any level; either professional or personal, and Dinah resented his attitude on both levels.

'Are you?' he insisted when she didn't answer, facing him in an angry silence.

'If I was, it wouldn't be any business of yours,' she muttered. Max Tracy couldn't hurt her any more but she felt a lancing pain under the hard blue stare of Quinn Howard's eyes. Her eyes burned with furious tears, she blinked, looking away.

'What was all that about the Adam Stuart programme? Was that his price for an affair with you? You sell yourself cheap—if you had held out, you might have got a proposal out of him.'

Dinah was so angry she shook with it; she picked up a book from the table and threw it at him. Quinn ducked, grabbed her by the shoulders and kissed her with ferocity, the fierce movement of his mouth making her lips burn and her head swim, an overwhelming sexual magnetism pulling her body weakly towards him although he exerted no pressure. Quinn's hand slid down her back and her spine arched; she hated herself for that instinctive response and used all her will power to break away, stumbling back from him.

Breathing thickly, Quinn turned to the door.

Dinah was shaking too much to notice anything about him, she leaned on the table with her head bent only half aware of the slam of the front door as he left. The intense desire inside her ached like an open wound; she hadn't wanted to push him away, she had hungered for much more than that insistent kiss but her self-respect wouldn't allow her to submit to lovemaking offered with such contempt. She seethed with all the things he hadn't waited to hear, her face deeply flushed.

Beth came into the room, eyeing her warily. 'Are you okay?'

'Do I look okay?' Dinah asked in hoarse rage and Beth studied her, then shook her head.

'You look like someone getting ready to break up the furniture,' she said with a grin half amused, half full of concern.

'Men make me sick!' Dinah told her.

'Join the club. What did Quinn say to make you go into a tailspin?'

'You should have heard him!'

'I did but it didn't make much sense—he was shouting too softly.' Beth looked at her watch. 'Here, I'm dying for some coffee—how about you?'

Dinah followed her into the kitchen, talking ferociously. 'And then he said I was cheap,' she ended and Beth whistled, pouring hot water on to coffee granules. Dinah was pacing the small room like a caged animal, scowling at everything she saw.

'I was surprised to see Max Tracy here, too, mind you,' Beth said with gentle insinuation. 'After all you'd said about him.'

'He came because he wants me to introduce him to Adam Stuart,' Dinah explained. 'I finally worked it out. I knew he was after something—I picked up the vibrations but I got them wrong. Today I guessed right and he admitted it.'

'What a creep,' Beth said, staring at her. 'But you still let him kiss you?' Her face was uncertain and Dinah grimaced at her.

'Well, it may sound stupid but I wanted to know how I'd feel if he did. When I met him again I couldn't help wondering if I still secretly felt the same.'

Beth looked amused. 'I can buy that. I think I'd be curious too. Old flames have a habit of smouldering, don't they? Isn't love funny? I wonder why we do it? Fall in love, I mean. Nature's little joke?'

'If that's what it is, I don't think much of nature's sense of humour.'

'Did it mean anything? Max's kiss, I mean?'

Dinah laughed suddenly, feeling very light-hearted. 'Not a damned thing. It was as exciting as kissing a maiden aunt. I felt sorry for him, that's all.'

'Sorry for him?' Beth was incredulous now, eyes round. 'You've got to be kidding.'

Dinah sipped her coffee, half smiling. 'But you know he is rather pathetic—fancy minding so much about getting a part, being ready to do anything to get it even when you know you've still only got a slim chance of succeeding. He wouldn't have bothered me at all if you hadn't told him about the Adam Stuart programme; then he plotted and planned to get back into my

good books in the hope that I might introduce
him to poor Adam Stuart. I wonder how many
people that man has to put up with, all trying to
get something out of him? It must make you very
cynical.'

'Another angle for you to tackle?' Beth asked.

Dinah sobered. 'If I'm still doing the programme. I don't know what Mark plans to do.'
She looked quickly at Beth. 'Do you? Has he
said anything?'

'Not to me,' Beth said. 'But then he wouldn't,
would he? Look, you should be back in bed. I'm
going to make the lunch—I've bought some trout
and I'll grill them, with a salad they should be
scrumptious, and I'll make a fruit salad of
oranges and peaches and strawberries. I got a
punnet very cheaply; we might as well have them
while they're in season. I'm taking a couple of
days off—I can study at home just as well and
who cares if I miss the odd lecture? It's nearly the
end of term, anyway.'

Dinah stood up without real reluctance. 'What
are you going to do this summer? Got any plans
yet?'

'Mark said he'd try to find me a part-time job,
he says there's always plenty of filing and typing
to do, especially during the summer when half
the secretaries are taking their annual holiday.'
Beth grinned at her wickedly. 'I hope Mark
doesn't suspect I'm using him the way Max
Tracy used you—I was quite frank about wanting
a job, I don't think he could misunderstand.'

'Men misunderstand everything,' Dinah said
cynically and went off to flop out on her bed,

letting her head empty of everything except a blissful sense of peace.

Mark came to see her next day. Dinah heard Beth's laughing voice and then the amused tone of Mark's replies, and sat up in bed, hurriedly pulling on her lace-trimmed bedjacket, grabbing her compact and making a few rapid improvements to her face and hair. She did not want Mark to see her looking like an invalid. She straightened the bed and looked at the door hopefully but he was taking his time to come in here. His conversation with Beth was apparently too fascinating to cut short. Dinah looked at the clock—he had been talking to Beth for ten minutes now. Perhaps he hadn't come to see *her* at all?

A moment later there was a tap on the door and Mark came in, smiling, but visibly self-conscious as he met Dinah's eyes. 'Hallo, how are you? Your nurse tells me you're a million times better but as we know she tends to exaggerate.'

'Not always,' Dinah said drily and Mark went faintly red.

'I gather she told you. About us, I mean about me and ... I know what you're thinking, you're probably right and I need my head examined.' He was standing at the foot of her bed looking as if he didn't know where to put himself and Dinah couldn't help smiling, she had never seen Mark look so helpless and uncertain of himself.

'You don't need to rehearse all the reasons why I shouldn't be seeing her,' he said, pushing his hands into his trouser pockets, rocking on his heels uneasily. 'I didn't intend . . . I don't know how it started.'

'I do,' Dinah said with wry amusement, and he looked at her with a startled expression, but she decided not to disillusion him. Mark was taking all the responsibility for the relationship and would probably deny any suggestion that Beth had prodded him into it. Dinah wasn't sure whether it was one-sided or not and she had decided not to interfere; Beth was so sure she knew what she was doing and whether she was fooling herself or not she had the right to make her own decisions.

'I'd rather you were frank,' Mark said. 'I know I'm much too old for her.'

Dinah frowned. 'If that's how you feel. . . .' Mark moved, sighing.

'That's the problem—I *feel* ten years younger when I'm with her, she makes me shed years. I haven't had so much fun for a long time. She's so full of life, she sparkles. It gives me a kick to spoil her, take her to new places—she enjoys it all so much, I feel that it's her who is taking me out. I'm discovering all sorts of new things. The other night we drove out into the country and had a drink at a small pub, it was wonderful.' He sat down on the bed, his head lowered, staring at the pile of magazines Dinah had been reading. 'She makes me happy, Dinah,' he said huskily and she was silent, not knowing what to say.

'Is it wrong?' Mark asked very quietly. 'Can it be wrong to be so happy?'

Dinah had to admit she simply didn't know. 'I suppose only time will tell. That's trite, I know, but nobody can answer that but you and Beth. It isn't fair to ask me a question like that. How can I say? Ask me again in ten years time.'

Mark said almost roughly: 'I'm not sleeping with her, you know.'

Dinah went pink. 'Mark, I didn't say you were—I wouldn't bring it up.'

He picked up one of the magazines and flipped over the pages without seeming to see them. 'Should I go down and meet your parents, do you think?'

'Up to you.'

'Do you think they'll hate me?'

'Don't be silly, why should they? They'll be worried, I can't say they won't. What's all the rush, though? Beth seemed to be prepared to take things slowly.'

'I haven't asked her to marry me,' Mark said and threw the magazine down. 'That wasn't what I meant. I just thought maybe I ought to tell her parents I'm dating her. I wouldn't like to be underhand about it. I didn't tell you because Beth asked me to keep quiet about it for a while, and I thought it might all fizzle out. I didn't think she would want to go on seeing me, I thought she was just curious and a bit intrigued. Once we got to know each other better, I imagined all the glamour would go out of it and she would lose interest. But she hasn't and the more I know her the more I enjoy being with her. I think we've got to the stage where we ought to let the rest of the world in on it, Dinah. If Beth isn't serious she won't be able to take how other people feel about it. I have to know that. About myself, as well as her. When people know. . . .'

His voice died away and he frowned. Dinah watched him with sympathy, recognising a genuine feeling in the way he had talked about Beth, the pain in his face now.

'You don't know if you can cope with people knowing?' she suggested and he spread his hands in an almost despairing gesture.

'You can imagine what they'll say.'

'Call you a cradle-snatcher?' Dinah said wryly and he looked at her sharply.

'I suppose so. Half the men will envy me and the other half will disapprove—it will depend whether they've got daughters or not. If they have, they'll take a personal interest and call me some unpleasant names.'

'Then you'd better find out as soon as possible,' Dinah said. 'If you can't take that sort of come-back the sooner you realise it the better.'

'Beth gets cross when I point that out to her, she's too young to realise how much it matters what the world thinks.'

'Or too self-confident to care what it thinks?'

Mark looked at her again, attentive to her tone. 'Tell me the honest truth, Dinah—do you think it could work out?'

'I've no idea, but I'm not the one you should be asking—ask Beth.'

Mark got up and walked to the window, fidgeting with the curtains. Dinah waited a few moments, then said: 'What about my programme? I feel fine now, I can come back to work tomorrow.'

Mark shook his head. 'You must have a longer

break than this—your nerves were far worse than I'd realised. There's no need to be ashamed of admitting it, everyone finds their work too much at times. I think you should take a week off and then see how you feel.'

'I'm doing the Adam Stuart interview next weekend. Mark, I want to do that one. I've spent weeks planning it, don't take it away from me.'

'We'll see—ask me again next Friday. In the meantime Quinn can take over for you and finish the Brixton interviews. There's very little to do, as far as I can see. I've been over your diary with Quinn and your secretary. There's nothing urgent that Quinn can't handle.'

Dinah sat tensely watching the back of his head. 'If I take this weekend off I'll be as right as rain by Monday.'

'No. I don't want to see you back in the office until next Friday at the earliest.' Mark walked to the door and she watched his restless, impatient movements with cold anger. She couldn't bear the idea of Quinn taking over her office, her programme, her ideas. She was intensely possessive about *One Nation*; it had been her brainchild from the beginning and she would rather see it taken out of the schedules than have it annexed by another producer, particularly Quinn Howard. He had been brooding overhead like a vulture for months, waiting for her to show signs of weakness, and now that she had faltered he was swooping down to snatch his prey. No doubt he was gloating over his triumph and all the other men would be cock-a-hoop too. She would have proved their case for them; she could kick herself for having let the tension build up inside her until it snapped with such uncontrolled violence.

'If you'd like to spend a few days at home, I'll drive you down there,' Mark said from the door. 'I'd like to meet your parents, they might as well be told about me and Beth. I'm free on Saturday if you feel up to the drive?'

Dinah nodded with dull resignation. 'Thanks.'

Mark gave her a sympathetic look, grinning comfortingly. 'Come on—it isn't that terrible! I'm giving you a week off work, not ordering your execution!'

He left and Beth came into the bedroom with a cup of tea and a biscuit. 'Not more food,' Dinah said crossly. 'Are you fattening me up for Christmas?'

Beth took the biscuit and bit into it. 'I'm sorry about your programme but it will be fun to see Mum and Dad, won't it?'

'Are you coming?'

'Of course—I'm not going to send Mark all alone, they might try to talk him into giving me up and I want to be there, to protect my interests.'

'And get your own way,' Dinah said bitterly. 'I feel sorry for Mark. He doesn't realise what a scheming female you are.'

Beth looked flattered. 'All's fair in love and war.'

'Which is this? It looks more like war than anything else. Mark is suffering pangs of conscience, you know.'

'I know,' Beth said with sudden grimness. 'He wants to protect me from himself, isn't it sweet?' She looked at Dinah, her arms laced behind her head and her slender body tense. 'Oh, Di, he is a darling and I'm crazy about him, I don't want anyone to spoil it. However guilty Mark feels because he's so much older, he doesn't want to give me up any more than I want him to. When I see him I feel . . .' she spread her arms, her eyes glowing, 'oh, wonderful!'

Dinah envied her but she couldn't help worrying about what the future might hold. Beth was trying to brush aside the problems but that wouldn't diminish them; the age gap between her and Mark held even greater problems in the future and Dinah knew her parents were going to be alarmed and distressed when they met Mark and were told that he and Beth were in love.

That evening she spent a lot of time watching television. One of the programmes had been produced by Quinn, working independently within the current affairs department. Dinah had to admire the sharpness of the focus, the tight way the programme had been put together. Quinn had a good mind and a flair for creative invention, much as she wished she could say otherwise.

Beth had gone out with Mark to see a new film which was opening in the West End that night; Mark often got tickets for first nights and previews, it was one of the perks of the job. Beth had hesitated about going, worried about leaving Dinah alone in the flat, but Dinah had scoffed at her anxiety. 'I'm quite capable of looking after myself, I'm not ill, just tired. Go with Mark, have a good time, I'll watch the TV and read and go to bed early.'

Dinah rang their parents to warn them that she and Beth were coming down that weekend and bringing Mark. Her mother was immediately flustered; fizzing with curiosity. 'Your boss, you mean? Is he going to stay?'

'No, he is driving us down but he will be driving straight back to London the same day.'

'Is he nice?' Her mother sounded slightly amused, her tone insinuated something and Dinah said guardedly that Mark was charming, they would like him.

'You've barely mentioned him in your letters,' her mother said with a faint reproach which baffled Dinah until she realised what it meant.

'I'm not dating Mark, Mum!' she protested. 'You're way off course.' She didn't feel she could jump the gun and give her mother a hint about Beth, though. 'I'm taking a week off because Mark thinks I need a rest, that's all.'

'What's wrong?' Mrs Sheraton asked at once, pouncing on the hint. 'Have you been ill?'

'No, just working too hard. Look, I'll tell you all about it when I see you. Bye.' Dinah hung up with a sigh of relief at having escaped the catechism she knew from experience would have followed. She looked at her watch, deciding it was time she made tracks for bed. There was nothing else she wanted to see on television and she might as well read comfortably in bed. Beth wouldn't be back for hours; she was going on to supper with Mark after the film. Grimacing, Dinah got up, feeling odd about going to bed at nine in the evening as if she was a child or an invalid.

She was making herself some cocoa when the doorbell rang and some sixth sense warned her that it was Quinn; she hesitated about answering it for a moment but he continued to ring insistently and she knew he would have seen the lights in the flat and be aware that someone was at home, so in the end she went to open the door.

Quinn looked as wary as she felt as they stared at each other. 'I was just planning to go to bed, can't you come back tomorrow?' she said in a tone dripping with cool courtesy.

'I only want the programme notes for the first two programmes in the series, Angela says you have them.'

She stiffened. 'Yes, I'm working on them at odd intervals and I can't see why you want them. Mark hasn't taken me off the series.' Yet, she thought grimly—he still might.

'Mark told me to familiarise myself with what you had planned and I can't do that without your notes.'

Quinn was using a new tactic, she noted; a remotely icy voice which matched the distance of his cool blue eyes. Dinah did not like it any more than she had liked his amusement, his irony, the constant needling he had subjected her to during the past two years.

'You might wait until Mark officially takes me off the series,' she bit out angrily, and Quinn's eyes narrowed.

'Has he said he's going to?'

'No, he hasn't, but that's what you're hoping for, isn't it?'

'Is it?' he asked in a voice like dry ice, staring

at her, those blue eyes running over the untidy mass of her auburn hair, her flushed and angry face, her slender body in the old blue jeans and American sweatshirt brought back from Los Angeles by a friend a year ago. Dinah hadn't bothered much with her appearance today; she hadn't been expecting visitors and had seen no point in putting on make-up or wearing anything but old clothes. Now she wished she had; she fidgeted under Quinn's appraising stare, her green eyes flashing.

'You used to be more direct; you didn't hide the fact that you wanted me off the series—why start pretending now?'

'I've tried every sort of approach, none of them seem to work,' Quinn threw back, frowning blackly. 'There seems little point, any more.'

'Because you've won,' Dinah said, breathing sharply. 'Is that what you think? Well, you can think again. I'm coming back on Friday and I'll fight like hell to keep my series in spite of you and all your friends. If you imagine I'm going to hand over to you without a struggle you're going to get a shock.'

Quinn's mouth compressed, his nostrils flaring. 'I still want those programme notes or do I need a written order from Mark before you'll hand them over?'

Dinah inhaled, suppressed the retort that rose to her lips and turned on her heel to walk into the sitting room. Quinn closed the front door and followed, hovering near the door as she picked up the files that lay on the table. She held them out to him, her hands shaking with a peculiar mix of emotions: anger, resentment, a deep sense of pain which was far more personal than professional. She did not want to lose her programme but it hurt far more to admit how much Quinn had affected her emotionally and how little he cared about her. He had finally got what he wanted and now he was icily indifferent to her; she hated him and felt a piercing sense of loss at the same time. Was she always going to be attracted to men who were so coldbloodedly ambitious?

Quinn took the files and looked down at them oddly, his mouth twisting. She saw the little grimace as one of triumph and wanted to cry, but she let the anger override that, she would not show him the hurt she felt.

'Well, you've got what you've wanted, now clear off and leave me alone,' she muttered, and Quinn turned and walked away.

CHAPTER NINE

DINAH followed like a defeated army, inwardly promising herself that this wasn't the end, she wasn't going to submit meekly to having her programme taken away, she couldn't believe that Mark seriously meant to do that to her. At the front door Quinn paused, giving her a cool flick of those blue eyes.

'I've got just one more thing to say to you, I was intending to keep quiet about it for a week or so but I've changed my mind, you might as well hear it now.'

She could guess what it was—he was going to explain to her again why she had been the wrong choice for an important series, why he was far more suitable and Mark was being wise in handing *One Nation* over to him. She didn't want to hear all that, she snarled at him viciously.

'I don't want to hear anything you have to say.'

'You never have wanted to,' he agreed with an anger which collided with her own and caused an explosion.

'You're so damned predictable! Why should I listen when I know exactly what you're going to say?'

'Do you?' He looked at her with violence. 'Do you? Even when you listened, you didn't hear what I was telling you. You wilfully misunderstood everything I ever said to you. I didn't want your damned programme, I still don't. . . !'

Dinah laughed bitterly, looking at the bulging files he was carrying under his arm. 'Of course not—that's why you can't even wait a week to grab my notes and start editing the film I've already shot.'

Quinn flung the files away with a savage movement; Dinah stared incredulously as paper fluttered everywhere like dying leaves, the air was full of handwritten sheets and photocopies of old newspaper cuttings. She went crimson with fury.

'What do you think you're doing? It will take hours to assemble all that in the right order!'

Quinn took not a scrap of notice, he was looking at her with barely controlled rage, breathing hard.

'I'm leaving Metro,' he broke out and Dinah froze, not believing her ears.

'What did you say?'

'I haven't officially told Mark yet although he knows I've applied for another job. I'll be giving in my notice on Monday and leaving in a month.'

Dinah was trembling, she needed to sit down. She walked through the sheaves of paper as though wandering through an autumn wood, her feet rustling and stirring the pages, and sat down heavily on the couch. Quinn stood in the doorway watching her without saying anything. She looked at him in bewilderment.

'But why?' Why was he leaving Metro just as he had achieved what he had been aiming for all these months? It didn't make any sense.

'I've been offered a job as head of current

affairs by one of our competitors,' he said flatly. 'Mark isn't too happy about it but he knows it is a big step-up, one I can't turn down—I would never earn that much money at Metro, the station is too small. I'll have better resources at my disposal and more scope for programme planning. The job has been on the table for a few months; the present guy is retiring in the autumn and they have been looking around for someone to take his place ever since the New Year. I know them quite well, I started with them years ago and I always wanted to go back some day, they're a good crowd. It isn't wise to stay anywhere for too long, though; you get into a rut and your work gets stale.'

She recognised the point of view he had expounded to her so many times in the past, and winced. Quinn was leaving Metro, he was going away, and she might never see him again. The thought struck her with a shock of pain, she looked at him and wished she hadn't jumped to so many wrong conclusions about him.

'I've always kept moving,' he said. She watched the lamplight gleaming on his skin as he turned his head, smiling wryly, and her heart was heavy.

'So you won't even be here to take over my series if Mark does take it away from me,' she said, almost to herself and felt him shift impatiently. She wasn't looking at him now but she had always been able to pick up each tiny change in him, either physical or mental. She had often misinterpreted them, but she was always aware of them.

'I never wanted to,' he said angrily. 'That was all in your head. You're too talented to waste your life on one programme at one small station, even if it is London-based. Mark won't thank me for saying this to you—but you ought to be moving on to bigger things. You've laid the foundation for a marvellous career but it is time you added a structure to it. There are dozens of opportunities for people as talented as you, Dinah—you could work abroad for a year, in America or Australia.'

She stiffened at the suggestion—if she was in another country on the other side of the world she would have no possible chance of seeing Quinn and she was dazed by a new realisation. Quinn had made himself a necessity to her; she might have been angry with him, she might have spent too much time quarrelling with him, but for a very long time, she had to admit, her days had revolved around him, life was dull if Quinn wasn't there to get into her hair and make her spit with fury. Saying goodbye to him would drain some of the colour out of her world, life would be black and white at best, and more probably grey.

'At least that would take you right away from Max Tracy,' Quinn said in a rough voice and her face washed with startled colour at the look in his eyes. 'He's no good for you—I don't understand how you can give a damn about him, and don't tell me that it isn't my business, you've made it plain that you can't stand the sight of me but I still have the right to. . . .'

When he stopped abruptly Dinah watched him tensely, her mouth dry. 'To what?' she prompted when he didn't go on.

Quinn moved away from the door, bent and pulled her to her feet, his hands compelling her towards him. 'To feel the way I do,' he said with a sort of savagery, staring at her face as she gazed back at him searching his features for some real clue as to what those feelings were, and defeated as always by the anger he wore like a mask. As if to confirm what her eyes told her, Quinn said: 'You make me so angry.'

'That hadn't escaped me,' Dinah said but with a lingering question mark in her voice. 'But I've often wondered why—if it isn't because you don't like women at the higher levels in production, or because you want my programme, why. . . .'

'Because of this,' Quinn said and his mouth came down to take hers in a hungry, searching exploration to which Dinah put up no defence for the first time; her lips parted and allowed the warm invasion, her arms went round his neck and clung, her body swayed closer until it pressed against his so that she could feel with every nerve the lean masculinity of the flesh so close to her own. She had her eyes shut, she could not see him, but her other senses were busy absorbing Quinn's reactions; the sudden quickening of his pulse, the harsh drag of his breathing, the heat of his skin as his kiss grew fiercer, more demanding, in response to her yielding mouth.

He moved his mouth across her face, kissing her cheekbones, her ears, her rounded chin. 'That's how I feel about you,' he muttered with his lips pressed into her throat. 'I tried to make it clear, God knows! Any woman with eyes in her head would have seen the obvious long ago.'

Dinah didn't want to break out of the smothering sweetness his lips were inflicting on her, the minute her lashes lifted and she saw his face she felt the old doubt and wariness. How could she risk caring about him when she knew how deceptive, how devious, men could be?

'It wasn't as obvious as you think.' Her breath caught in her throat and she couldn't go on as Quinn's hands beseiged her senses, one of them inside her sweatshirt, making her skin shiver with pleasure as his fingers slid between her bra and her warm flesh, while the other held her buttocks, caressing the contours of their firm pressure against her jeans.

'I almost spelled it out for you,' Quinn said wryly, his teeth gently nibbling at her earlobe, the tiny caress discreet enough but those exploring hands far too confident, each movement they made a new attack on her weakening defences. Dinah was trying to think, but how could she when he was doing such dangerous things to her metabolism? Her blood was running fast and hot, she couldn't breathe properly, her lungs snatched at air as though she were under water and in danger of drowning, her breasts had filled with that heated blood, her tissues swollen, aching with desire as his delicate fingers teased her nipples.

'I thought. . . .' she began and he inserted his tongue into her ear, following the whorled shell softly. 'Oh,' Dinah breathed, her eyes closing again. She staggered backwards and overbalanced on to the couch, taking Quinn with her.

'You were always laughing at me!' she

protested and he framed her face in his hands and looked at it through half-closed eyes, a dark flush on his cheeks.

'You're very funny,' he admitted but there was no humour in his narrowed eyes. What she saw in them made her breathe much faster. 'You're quick-witted, not to say vicious with that tongue of yours.' His gaze dwelt on her mouth and she shuddered. He caressed her lips with the tip of his own tongue, making a noise in his throat, a warm purring that was intensely sexy. 'You're beautiful, too,' he whispered and she held him away, a hand on his chest.

'You refused to take me seriously, though!'

'I was always ready to take you, and believe me—I was serious!' She slapped his hand away as he fingered the zip of her jeans, her flush hectic.

'Never mind the double meanings! Why have you sniped and sneered at me for months?'

His face changed, becoming tense. 'I've never sneered at you—I admire your intelligence and your talent, how could you imagine I didn't? You're a brilliant programme maker with an original mind, I like the way you look at life, I agree with most of your opinions on society. You're a very impressive lady, Dinah—as a colleague I respect you a great deal.' His eyes were clear and steady, unwavering in their direct stare. She couldn't read any hidden meanings, any ulterior motives in them now. 'As a woman, though, you made me anxious—you were spending yourself too fast, throwing everything you were into your work. You don't seem to realise that there's a limit to what you give, you're generous and reckless and I was afraid for you. If I sniped at you it was because you worried me so much. I tried everything I knew to make you see the dangers you were running.'

'You were too oblique, then,' Dinah muttered. 'I was used to the other men sniping because they wanted me out of Metro—when you started doing it, I naturally thought you felt the same way.'

'There's nothing natural about it,' Quinn said. 'They find you terrifying; they're a pretty mediocre collection and mediocrity always resents an original mind, especially when it challenges them. Your programme was different and they can't forgive you for that. Don't class me with them, Dinah—I don't find you terrifying, you make me feel twice as alive, you're a challenge I can't resist.' He looked at her mouth, his blue eyes hooded by lids which left only a brooding slit of intent observation visible. His hand travelled tormentingly over her thighs and Dinah caught it, held it, shaking her head at him.

'Will you stop that?'

'No,' he said, smiling. 'You don't want me to.'

'Oh, don't I? Who says?'

'I do,' he told her with maddening assurance. 'If you don't want me to make love to you, stop looking at me like that.'

'Like what?' she asked trying to control her treacherous expression.

He tugged at his tie and took it off, opening his shirt while she watched with a sense of raging uncertainty; Quinn was calmly forcing the pace and Dinah wasn't ready to make up her mind yet.

She was fighting a rearguard action against
herself as much as him, reluctant to be trapped in
a painful relationship with another ambitious
man. Quinn might be leaving Metro, he might be
giving up any plan he had had of getting her job,
but she was afraid to trust him with her heart.
Hearts might not break but they could bruise;
love didn't kill anyone but it could leave them
badly scarred.

'If I had a mirror I'd show you how you're
looking at me,' Quinn said with that mockery that
had always infuriated her.

'You're too clever, I don't trust you,' Dinah
said, frowning.

'For God's sake hold your tongue and let me
love,' Quinn muttered in a suddenly husky
voice, his bare throat moving convulsively as he
swallowed; and the emotion in his voice was too
ragged to be assumed, the turmoil in his
darkening eyes too violent to be pretence. She
trembled, her hand against his chest to hold
him back as he moved closer. Under her palm
his skin pulsed with urgency and his eyes
moved over her with flickering excitement.
'Love now, talk later,' he said and kissed her
with a force that was almost brutal in its
insistence. Dinah closed her eyes and closed the
questioning valves of her intelligence that would
not let her surrender to the clamour of her
senses. She shut off everything but the incredible pleasure Quinn was offering her; to
that she was so intensely sensitive that she
almost cried out, her whole body burning as his
mouth and hands tormented her. She needed to

touch him, discover his body with the same freedom.

'I love you,' Quinn groaned, sliding her jeans downward without any resistance from her. His hand ran over her naked, supple body and she closed her arms around his back, arching to that touch. 'I've been dying to do this,' he said, pulling her down on to the carpet in a smooth tangle of limbs which like some living geometry began to form strange, complex structures which melted one into the other; the rounded curve of her hip below the angularity of his, the cone of her breast flattened by the flat wall of his chest, the two dark triangles welding together and his hair prickling the sensitive flesh of her inner thigh.

'I must be mad,' Dinah thought aloud, arching beneath him with her knees gripping his waist and her hands clasping his back.

'A little madness makes for sanity,' Quinn said wryly.

She wasn't really listening, she was tuned to the vibrations his wandering hand set up inside her as it followed the deep indentation it had found; a moist heat prickled beneath his fingertips and a groan came from deep within her throat. She was abruptly urgent, her hands pressed him down and Quinn entered her, the hard flesh entombed in receptive clinging warmth, Dinah's long gasp of relief echoed by his sigh. His hands went under her, raising her, he moved gently at first, rocking her with the slow thrusts. His mouth incited, his tongue tip running over her nipples, his lips pressing into the pulsing flesh of her throat. Dinah's face was on his bare shoulder, she parted her lips and closed them on his flesh, sucking, tasting the faint salt on his skin. Quinn gave a little groan of pleasure and she bit him gently, conscious of the fine hair dusting his skin and roughening as it spread into a wedge up the centre of his chest. Her hand slipped down his back and followed the downward curve of his buttocks, her fingertips brushing and teasing. The deliberate leash on which he held them both snapped; Quinn's breathing thickened, his thrusts quickened and drove into her with a force that made her body jerk convulsively as she held on to him.

Her mind clouded, she lost all sense of everything but this powerful rhythm, the gallop of his muscled body riding her until the whole of existence seemed to be centred on the clamouring throb of her hidden flesh, closing and opening on the intruder, moist as some sea creature engulfing a prey, red as the heart of a rose. Deeper and deeper he struck and her breath hurt as she gasped, her head turned from side to side, frantic for release from the exquisite tension, her skin stretched too tightly over her taut bones and aching.

Her nails dug into his back as she arched upward, crying out. The veins in her neck stood out, her head fell back on to the carpet and her desire hit a peak of such intensity that she stifled her wild cries on Quinn's chest.

When she could see and hear again she looked up at him, very hot. 'Well, well,' he said huskily. 'Did I call you cold? You've been hiding things from me.'

She lay under him so totally relaxed that she was limp, her body drained of tension, her skin burning. He brushed back a tangle of auburn hair, smiling. 'Good, was it?'

Dinah was shy now; she looked down, biting her lip. 'Beth may come back soon, we must get dressed.'

'She won't be back for another hour at least. Did I tell you I loved you?'

He was kissing her as he said it and Dinah kissed him back uncertainly. 'You're heavy,' she said as she disentangled her lips.

'Say it,' Quinn whispered, his hand intimately moving downward.

'I don't know,' she said in a distraught murmur and he laughed.

'You seemed sure enough a minute ago.'

'That isn't fair.' It was so long since her body had experienced that fierce sensual pleasure; it would be too easy to confuse desire with love. She couldn't pretend she did not want him, she would never convince him now that she didn't, but to say 'I love you' was a commitment she was afraid to make.

'You said it then,' Quinn told her and she stared at him, not remembering what she had said, her tongue had been clamouring as fiercely as her body, she had had no control over either. Quinn's face was odd, she couldn't remember seeing him in any mood where he was not totally sure of himself but now he looked so uncertain, so hesitant, his blue eyes hunting for assurance in hers, his mouth not steady. She felt a queer little tremor of emotion which was not passion; it was concern, affection, a caring instinct which was new to her. She wanted to smooth out the lines in his forehead, bring back that lazy smile, restore his confidence in himself.

'I need you to love me,' Quinn said, his voice deep and shaken.

Dinah held him, cradling him. 'Then I suppose I must,' she said feeling self-conscious.

'Don't be flip, Dinah, not now,' he said with a sort of groan. 'Do you think I like running the risk of making a fool of myself? You're very special to me; don't make a joke of it.'

'I love you,' she said, kissing him hurriedly so that she need not meet his eyes, but he held her head away, forcing her to look at him, searching her face for assurance and very flushed she gave it to him, as she had given him her body a moment ago, reluctantly and yet with total abandonment in the end.

Quinn's eyes cleared, glowed. 'Once more— with feeling,' he said with that old mockery and she said what he wanted to hear. What did it matter in the end whether the future stretched on endlessly or finished tomorrow? She was happy here and now and this present happiness was worth any risk.

'I love you, damn you,' she said and Quinn closed his eyes briefly.

'Now that sounds real,' he whispered. 'So much for the signature on the contract—but what about the small print? Show me!' His body moved and she laughed helplessly.

'I just did.'

'Darling, you were so busy enjoying yourself

that it may have escaped your notice, but that time was for you. Now it's my turn.'

'Oh,' she said, taken aback.

'You really didn't know? My God, just wait . . . you won't make any mistake when it happens,' Quinn said with wicked amusement.

It was another hour before they dressed and sat together on the couch drinking coffee and talking with a contented weariness, Quinn's arm around her and her head on his shoulder.

'I thought I'd never get through to you,' Quinn said. 'You've been giving me a bad time.'

'What do you think you've been doing to me?'

'You didn't have to worry about any other women, ever since I found out about you and that Tracy guy I've been afraid you were going to take up with him again.'

'I'd be crazy if I did; Max is only interested in one thing.'

'That's what I was afraid of,' Quinn said, his hand sliding over her shoulder to cup her breast with possessive fingers.

Dinah laughed, touching his hand, stroking the splayed fingers. 'Not that,' she said. 'Max is only interested in Max.'

'Yes, that figures,' he agreed. 'He's an actor—what do you expect?' He kissed her ear. 'What are we going to do? We're both going to be very busy and I don't want to have to make do with dinner together once in a blue moon and maybe the odd weekend. I want you in my bed every night and breakfast together would be fun, too.'

'Is this a proposal or a proposition?' Dinah challenged and he shrugged lazily.

'Up to you. We could get married or live together first and then get married, I'm putty in your hands.'

'That's a joke,' Dinah said, but thinking hard. 'Marriage is a big step.'

'We can always sleep on it,' Quinn said teasingly and she laughed.

'You have a tortuous mind. My flat or yours?'

'Mine's bigger and I don't have a sister cluttering up the place,' Quinn said as Beth's key turned in the lock of the front door. She came into the sitting room with Mark a few seconds later. They rustled as they came, staring down at the script pages littering the corridor, frowning and looking very worried. Dinah would have moved out of Quinn's embrace but his hand coerced her; she stayed where she was and Mark and Beth looked from the paper-strewn floor towards the couch, their eyes widening in surprise but the anxiety leaving their faces.

'What have you two been doing? Playing paper chases?' Mark enquired, starting to laugh.

'Dinah?' Beth asked, staring, fascinated and round-eyed.

'I won't ask who was chasing who and who got caught,' Mark added drily. 'It all depends on the point of view, I suppose.'

Quinn grinned, stretching his loose-limbed body and holding on to Dinah with one arm. 'Beth, take Mark away and make him some coffee, Dinah doesn't appreciate his sense of humour.'

'Do you want some?' Beth asked obediently

steering Mark out of the room.

'I've got all I want, thank you,' Quinn said with calm satisfaction and as the door closed he turned Dinah's head his way and began to kiss her again.

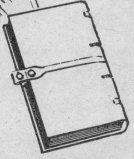

EXPERIENCE

Harlequin Temptation ™.

Sensuous...contemporary...compelling...reflecting today's love relationships! The passionate torment of a woman torn between two loves...the siren call of a career ...the magnetic advances of an impetuous employer–nothing is left unexplored in this romantic new series from Harlequin. You'll thrill to a candid new frankness as men and women seek to form lasting relationships in the face of temptations that threaten true love. *Don't miss a single one!* You can start new *Harlequin Temptation* coming to *your* home each month for just $1.75 per book–a saving of 20¢ off the suggested retail price of $1.95. Begin with your FREE copy of *First Impressions*. Mail the reply card today!

First Impressions
by Maris Soule

He was involved with her best friend! Tracy Dexter couldn't deny her attraction to her new boss. Mark Prescott looked more like a jet set playboy than a high school principal–and he acted like one, too. It wasn't right for Tracy to go out with him, not when her friend Rose had already staked a claim. It wasn't right, even though Mark's eyes were so persuasive, his kiss so probing and intense. Even though his hands scorched her body with a teasing, raging fire...and when he gently lowered her to the floor she couldn't find the words to say no.

A word of warning to our regular readers: While Harlequin books are always in good taste, you'll find more sensuous writing in new *Harlequin Temptation* than in other Harlequin romance series.
® ™Trademarks of Harlequin Enterprises Ltd.